Thirsty

by

Joyce Dicus

ISBN: 1-60388-797-0
978-1-60388-797-7

Contents

Chapter 1

She lay on the bed thrashing about and moaning. The fever that raged through her body was leaving her parched and dry. Her skin was already so hot to touch that even the sheet that she lay on felt like a warming pad. Her lips were cracked and the inside of her throat was so dry that it felt like it was stuck together. She drew in deep, ragged breaths and sometimes she shivered. It had been this way since early yesterday morning, when she had awakened with those grievous sores all over her body. The antibiotics, when she could keep them down, had not helped that, anymore that the aspirin and the Tylenol had helped to reduce the fever. She felt herself growing weaker by the moment. She wanted a good cold glass of water so badly that she would gladly beg or maybe even kill for it. Even the tepid tap water from the rusty old pipes in the kitchen sink would taste like Heaven. With extreme effort, after several tries, she finally hauled herself from the bed, and by holding onto the furniture, she made it into the kitchen. She dropped the first glass that she picked up and watched it shatter on the kitchen floor. Mindful of her bare feet, she got another one from the cabinet and turned on the tap. For a second, nothing happened, and then a slow drop or two of water fell into the sink. As the drops turned into a trickle, they also turned red. At first, it was a very faint red, barely more than pink. In her fevered state, she thought that she must have cut her hand and somehow gotten some blood in the water. Setting the glass aside, she checked for an injury. There wasn't one. Puzzled, she looked back at the faucet, which now issued a full stream of what looked like pure blood. When she tentatively stuck her finger in the stream, it even felt warm and sticky like blood. She jumped back in horror, completely forgetting the glass on the floor and the danger of cutting her bare feet.

She screamed and came awake with a jolt, sitting straight up in her bed. As she sat there shaking, she felt of her skin. It was cool. She looked at her body, expecting sores, but found only the minor scratches from her walk in the woods yesterday. The dream had been so real. She was still shaking. Not for the first time, she found herself wishing that she wasn't so alone in the world. There was no one there to offer comfort, no arms to hold her and no gentle voice to tell her that it was only a dream.

If someone had been there, she wouldn't have

believed them anyway. It was far too realistic to be just a dream. When she finally stopped shaking and went to the kitchen to make her coffee, she was almost afraid to turn the water on. Her breathing became normal at last when the faucet yielded only water and she made her coffee as usual. She sat at the table and sipped it a little longer than normal, then had to rush to get to work. Staying home was not an option, no matter how shaken she was, she had obligations to meet and bills to pay. She was not a stranger to dreams, but this dream was far worse than even the prophetic dreams that she used to have back in the days when she went to church. They had frightened her, but not like this.

Pushing the memories of how her life used to be out of her mind, she got dressed and brushed her hair. As she grabbed her car keys and headed out of the house, she couldn't help but glance at the small pond to see if the water was red or blue. She dreaded going to work today. There was a time when she would have loved it. She turned on the radio as she backed out of the driveway. The news was depressing. There had been more terrorists attacks overnight and there was more loss of lives of American soldiers in the aftermath of the war with Iraq. Before the war, she was not even aware that Iraq was near the area that used to be named Babylon. She felt shivers shoot up her spine as she thought of all the prophecy about Babylon in the Bible and she couldn't help but wonder if it was beginning now. She forced her mind back onto what the announcer was saying. There was another suicide bombing in Israel. After that, he told of numerous murders and bank robberies closer to home. There were all kinds of protests going on in Washington DC. She eased her new car into a parking space then just sat there and took a deep breath, dreading going in and starting the workday, dreading facing the people. Somewhere deep inside, she knew that she should be grateful that she had a business of her own, when some folks didn't even have a job. She should be enjoying her new car, but somehow the new things didn't make her happy. No matter what she bought or how many materialistic things she accumulated, something was still missing. She hated being alone. There seemed to be no reason for anything. Nothing seemed to fill the empty spot that was always there, deep inside her. It tormented her, just like that thirst that never went completely away. With these thoughts running through her mind and her head hung down, she walked toward the store.

"Good grief Ella! What on earth is wrong with you? You look like death warmed over!" Sue had her arms stretched out like she thought Ella might fall and she'd have to catch her.

Ella jumped. Secluded in her own little world, and lost in worry and depression, she had not seen Sue get out of her car and follow her to the door. Her mind was still on the dream, or nightmare, or what ever it was that plagued her last night. She noticed the people on the sidewalk starring at her, and when she glanced in one of the display mirrors, she could see why.

Her complexion, which was usually healthy and bright, was now very pale with a grayish tint. She wished that she had taken a few minutes to put on a little make up. The grayish color and the dark circles under her big brown eyes made her look like an alien from outer space. The frown on her face that she just couldn't seem to get rid of didn't help either. It was enough to make any potential customer turn and run away. Without answering, Ella headed straight to the back of the building and busied herself by stocking the shelves, putting items out to go in the display window, and checking materials. Her behavior was so disturbing today that no one seemed to know what to say or do. Usually, when she was at the store, she was filled with nervous energy, and tended to talk too much, and she always tried to put on a friendly face for the public. She was so quick to spout off whatever came to mind that people often joked that she was crazy. Maybe they really believed it. Sometimes she did. It was hard to remember the days when she was quite, even shy. She'd been making a lot of progress, but now, once again, she wanted to run away and hide.

Sue, who was her best friend, best customer, and was closer than any flesh and blood sister could ever be, still followed her, but Ella remained silent, lost in thought. She wasn't really sure that she could talk to anyone today, not even to Sue. Usually, they could finish each other's sentences and at times, even seemed able to communicate without words. Sue wasn't one to give up. She just didn't have it in her to walk away when something was wrong with someone she loved, and Ella didn't think that there was anyone on Earth that Sue didn't love.

"Are you sure you're not sick? If you need to go see a doctor, or just want to go home and get some rest, I can manage the store for you. I know you've got that shipment coming in today, but I can handle it." Concern was written all over Sue's face.

"No thanks. I just had a bad night. Couldn't sleep, had a really bad dream." She winced at the memory and started the coffee maker. That was all Ella could manage to say. She felt like her throat would stick together before she got that out.

"Must have been some nightmare." Sue gave her a strange look as she finally gave up and walked away. When she glanced back over her shoulder one more time, with a puzzled look on her face, Ella wanted to run after her and tell her that she was sorry. Instead, she gulped down the coffee. A few minutes later, Ella heard Sue talking and laughing with two other women that had entered the store. Soon she heard the sound of the old cash register as Sue made the first sale of the day. She didn't know what she would do without Sue to lean on and prayed silently that she'd never have to find out.

Ella stayed at the back of the building, hiding. It felt natural. Existing was all she'd really been doing for the last few months anyway, until she was forced to find a job, and then later she'd opened the store. She had survived by staying very busy, trying not to think about herself. Now, she found herself wanting to run away and hide again, distance herself even more from everything and everyone that she knew. For a moment, she thought about going to Nashville and living with the homeless, just giving up on life, then wondered where such a crazy thought came from. She knew she couldn't do that. There was Betsy and Daniel to think about. They were her life now, her only reason for living. There was no escape, no running away. She'd tried that already.

Out of nowhere, the verses in Psalms 139 entered her mind. She couldn't quote it word for word, but she knew what it was all about. It basically said there was no hiding place, that God knew her, what she did, said, and thought. It didn't matter if it was dark or light, or where she went. There was no escape. She remembered a time when that was a comfort, but not now. She even felt isolated from Him. She ached for the closeness that she used to have with God. She missed that even more than she missed her husband, John.

"Bingo!" She knew where the dream had come from. Revelations. The things yet to come. She could see Matthew 24 happening every day. All that she had to do was turn on the television. Tears formed and threatened to spill over. Her thoughts turned to the past. It seemed like a lifetime ago that she was a happy wife and a mother, and grandmother. She was still a mother and a grandmother, reminding herself of that helped a little. It was the best part of her life, even if her daughter seemed to be growing more independent and self-reliant and more distant with each passing day. Her grandson was almost a teenager now, and so big for his age. He was also growing away from her and spending more time with his little group of friends. He would start junior high next year. It didn't seem possible. She understood that all of this was a healthy and normal process, but it sure wasn't easy to let go, especially now. A part of her wanted to grab hold of them both and hold on for dear life, but she reminded herself that she didn't have her child just to keep her in a closet or tied to her apron strings. She certainly wasn't the type to try and relive her own life through her child. She had seen people who had given up their own lives to take care of their aging or disabled parents, and she surly did not want that for her child. She knew that she had to let Betsy and Daniel live their own lives, give them their freedom. Still, she missed them so very much. She'd never felt so alone, or so thirsty. She refilled the coffee cup. Memories that she tried hard to suppress flooded her mind.

Betsy and Daniel had stuck to her like glue the first two weeks after John had died. The three of them had huddled together and cried for hours, remembering all the good times and forgetting the bad. The funeral was a horrible experience. John's brother, Jack had made a scene. It had been a trying time for everyone. Jack had blamed Ella for John's heart attack, shouted it out at the funeral home in front of about fifty people.

Healing and acceptance had barely started, when they found out about the will. They discovered that John had left the house and almost everything else to his brother, giving Ella a lifetime dowry. It seemed like a nightmare or a cruel joke. Ella was shocked! She just couldn't believe that it was real. She didn't think anything like that could really happen. She was his wife! Wasn't it part her house too?

Ella had worked as hard as anyone to build their home and their life together. She had thought of it as theirs, not just his. True, everything had been in Johns' name. He had been the boss of the family, definitely the head of the household in every way, but she couldn't believe that he had done this to her. She had always been there in the background, backing him up, sometimes holding him up. He had no right to treat her this way. She didn't even think it was legal. Surely it wasn't. Hurt turned to anger and then she felt guilty because John was dead. She pounded her pillow and cried at night because John wasn't there for her to pound. Guilt, grief and anger battled inside her.

She couldn't help it; anger finally won out over her grief. Ella was furious! She was more than furious! She paced the floor and wrung her hands and wondered what on earth she was going to do. She wondered why on earth John would give their home to Jack. She remembered the farm they had sold to buy the house in town.

She had hammered as many nails and hoisted as many two-by-fours as he had when they built that barn. She had stretched as much wire and set as many fence posts as he had. They had spent many weekends working side by side like that. Ella was the one that fed the animals and cared for them seven days a week. She kept up with the profits and loss and she did all this until finally, he had sold the old farm that they had bought from John's parents and moved to the outskirts of town, a little subdivision barely inside the city limits. She remembered how happy Betsy had been to be near other children and how proud they both were of the modest brick house that had so quickly become home. Ella had remained mostly a loner, maybe even become more of one, since she didn't have the animals for company, but Betsy had flourished and John had gotten a raise. She knew in her heart that she was happier too, because it had always been hard for her when the animals were sold. No matter how hard she tried not to think of it, she knew that they would be slaughtered for meat.

John had been a sales representative for a pharmaceutical company based out of Jackson. That part of his life was seldom shared with Ella. He worked long hours and was on the road a lot. Usually, he wouldn't make it home one or two nights a week and he always complained about having to stay in motels, but when he was home he was treated like a king. No man had ever been more loved. Ella had thought the feeling mutual. She had felt loved and protected and had not even realized that her husband felt so superior to her, that he had some how felt and convinced everyone he knew that she was not capable of managing on her own. He had mistaken love and devotion for weakness.

At least John had left their daughter twenty thousand dollars and there was a life insurance policy on him that was made out to Ella, which had just covered his burial expenses. If Jack had gotten his hands on that, he would have used it for something else. Ella had always known that John was old fashioned when it came to women, but she had not minded that. Now she berated herself. She should never have been so trusting. She should have been better prepared. She should never have lived her life in John's shadow. How could she have been so blind? She wasn't stupid, but she had been almost invisible. Most of the plans and ideas that had made them a successful family had been hers. She had just let John take all the credit for them. She had never imagined a life without him.

She had always known how much he loved his younger brother, and Jack had also known this and had used John something awful. He 'borrowed' money and never paid it back. He got John to co-sign notes for him and then John had to pay them off because Jack didn't. It was almost like John had to support two households. Jack got behind on his rent and had to move often, but John never complained about any of it. When money was short, Ella didn't even ask. She just knew that it had gone to Jack.

John had been blind to his brother's faults. Anything that Jack wanted, John tried to help him get. It was the one thing that they had argued about. Ella had accused him of loving Jack more than he loved his own child. Well, she had certainly been proven right about that. Jack had been a thorn in her side since the first day they met. She knew that he would waste no time in taking possession of the house and there was no way that she could live in the same house with him and his family. She knew that she had to do something.

She couldn't remember a time when she didn't love John. They had married when she was just seventeen, barely out of high school. She had her only child when she was eighteen, and gradually lost all sense of her own life and dreams. In many ways, she had been sheltered and protected. John had taken care of all the bills. He had been the visible breadwinner, the head of the family in every sense of the word. She had let him be the boss, partly because it was easier to let him do things his way than to fight about it. Everyone always said how lucky she was to have a man like John to take care of her. She had thought so too.

Ella had been happy staying at home and taking care of her daughter. Betsy was a delight, but like her mother before her, she was married and had a child of her own by the age of eighteen. John never quite got over the fact that their only child was not a boy. He really didn't believe that a woman should be anything other than a wife and mother. He thought that men were the providers and protectors of the world. He cared more about his baby brother, Jack, than he did about his daughter, treating him like the son they'd never had. John was sixteen years older than his little brother. All his life, John's parents had drilled it into his head that it was his place to take care of Jack. It was a responsibility that John had loved.

John was never very close to Betsy's son, Daniel. He complained that he was too much of a mama's boy. Daniel didn't like being around Jack and it was easy to see that he resented the way that his grandfather treated his mother and grandmother. Daniel had a healthy respect for all women, especially his mom. Still, it was a good life until John suddenly dropped dead from a heart attack and their world fell apart.

The day had started out perfectly normal. John was talking about his plans for the weekend while he dressed for work and Ella cooked breakfast. While he was sitting at the breakfast table, he suddenly got a frightened look on his face. Suddenly, he grabbed his chest with both hands, took one deep breath, and fell out of his chair.

"John!" Ella knocked her own chair over in her haste to get to him, but it didn't matter, for he was already dead by the time that he hit the floor. She called 911 and then she called Betsy. The five minutes that it took the ambulance to get there seemed like five years. John was pronounced dead on arrival at the hospital. A massive coronary, they were told, was the cause of death. Nothing could have saved him; still, Ella beat herself up for not knowing CPR.

Ella and the kids were in shock. John was only fifty-eight years old. He had always been so healthy. They had never talked about death or wills or anything on that order. That's why Ella was so surprised to find out that John had made one six years ago. She was even more surprised when she found that John had left almost everything that they owned to his brother. She had not even realized that her name was not on the deed. When she found out that Jack got their house and almost everything that they had accumulated over the years, and Ella got a life time dowry, she went to see the lawyer. She was told that if she had money, she could fight it, but that there was no guarantee that she would win. She had never held a job and she barely had a high school education, the lawyer explained. Her name wasn't on the deed. The farm had belonged to John's parents before it belonged to John. He had sold that to buy the house. Still she didn't accept it until Jack and his wife and kids started moving their belongings into the house. They did this a little at a time, but told her that they would be completely moved in by the weekend when Jack could get a few friends to help him with the heavy stuff. They moved Ella's stuff to the back bedroom, and when she protested, Jack reminded her that it was his house now, and while he had to let her stay, he was boss. She stood there with her mouth open and he smiled and walked out the door.

That's when the shock and grief left and anger took its place. Ella took what money she had hidden away for household expenses and what little she had hoarded over the years and rented a storage space. She moved her sewing machine and everything else that she could haul in her old station wagon to the little storage building. By some miracle, the old station wagon that she drove was in her name and Jack couldn't touch it. She had no intentions of living in her own home as a poor relation to Jack. When he moved in, she was moving out! She tried to talk to her daughter, but that was a big mistake.

Betsy, who was still in shock and grieving over the loss of her dad, really didn't understand what was going on. She was so hurt that talking to her just made everything worse. She was just getting her marriage back on track and then she had been hit with the death of her father. Mother and daughter were both hurting so badly that they couldn't comfort each other.

"How on earth can you be so worried over money and houses and things when Daddy just died?" Betsy glared at her mother. "Get over it Mom! It's not all about you," she yelled as she stormed out the door.

Ella felt sorry for herself and she hurt for her daughter. Betsy really couldn't help anyway; it would have just caused more problems in her own marriage. She and Rob were just now getting over a very rough spot and Ella certainly didn't want to move in with them. She could see how badly her daughter was hurting. She'd find a way to cope on her own. She didn't know how to help Betsy. She didn't even know how to help herself. All their lives had fallen apart and she wondered what on earth she was she going to do. Where would she find a place to live or money for rent? She found herself just driving around and thinking a lot of the time. Because she had little money for gas, she would often park in isolated places and just sit there for hours.

Jack and his family were completely moved in by the first of the week and Ella just couldn't bring herself to go home. She tried to. Reason told her that she had to. There was nowhere else to go, but she just couldn't do it. She even drove by the house several times, but she just couldn't make herself stop. She just kept on driving until she was outside the city limits in an isolated area near the place where she once lived. It was getting dark, and she pulled the car off the main road onto an old logging road that was no longer being used. She spent that night and several more sleeping in her car.

Actually, the old station wagon was big and comfortable and she had a small mattress and plenty of quilts and pillows still stacked in the back seat. There had not been enough room for them in the storage building. When she folded the back seat down and placed the quilts and pillows, it made a comfortable bed. She fell asleep listening to the sound of the insects singing, or the wind blowing through the trees. She lived this way for weeks and no one knew it. Jack and June must have thought that she was with Betsy and Betsy thought that she was at home. They were all dealing with their own loss and their own hurt, but Ella felt that no one really cared.

Outside the little town in the rural area where she'd lived most of her life, there were plenty of old logging roads and trails and she could always find a different isolated spot to pull off and park for the night. She wasn't afraid, she had grown up in the country, surrounded by woods. She could spend hours just sitting on the side of the river bank thinking, planning, or dreaming. She had always been a loner and she managed to keep her situation a secret without much effort. Still, she knew that she had to find a place to live before people found out. Evidently, John had led everyone to believe that she was mentally deficient. She had to do something. If anyone found out how she was living, they might try to have her committed. It upset her to think that people thought her retarded due to the lifestyle that she had lived. She knew that she couldn't hide and lick her wounds forever. She didn't know of any other homeless people around these parts, but she could not live with Jack and for different reasons, she couldn't live with Betsy. She started to formulate different plans in her mind.

She needed a job, but had few skills, no references, and no job experience. She couldn't baby sit because she didn't have a decent place for children to stay and she didn't want to go into someone else's home to work. They'd ask questions and check references and find out that she was homeless. She could clean houses, but she had little money for supplies and no place to keep them. There was no way that she was going to store cleaning products, especially liquids, in the storage building nor in the car with the sun shinning down and causing so much heat. References would be a problem with that also. She had no phone number for potential clients to call her. She could sew, but she also had no place to do that. She could cook! She was a very good cook. There were plenty of restaurants in town and they always needed help. A physical and a TB skin test would probably be all she'd need for that. She would just not tell them of any changes. She would rent a post office box so that she would have an address.

Hohenwald was a very small town and jobs were few, but they had plenty of restaurants! Most of the plants had closed down or moved away, but Ella loved it here. She always had. She remembered when she was nine years old and her family had moved back to Tennessee from California. They drove through Hohenwald and she had asked her mother if Hohenwald was a village. It was the smallest town that she had ever seen. Things had changed a lot since then, but it was still a very small town. Hohenwald is a German word and it means 'city of the high forest'. It was true that from any direction that you entered the town, you had to come up a hill.

Ella got a job cooking in a restaurant. The day that she applied, they were short of help and they put her right to work. She was a hard worker and it helped to stay busy. She learned how to operate the cash register, as well as everything else that she thought would help her start a new life. To her surprise, she found that she enjoyed talking and interacting with the customers. Three weeks later, when she got her first paycheck, she rented an old run down trailer that really should have been condemned. She had found it by accident while she was hiding out and living in her car. It was in an isolated location, just the kind of place that she loved. It was surrounded by trees and was only about a mile from the beautiful, scenic

Buffalo River. The trailer faced the road and had a big front yard. There was an old garden, grown up with weeds and surrounded by a falling down fence off to one side and the other side and the back was a forest. There was a small pond at the end of the field. She asked around and found that the place belonged to a woman named Sue Ainsloy, who lived in the big, white house about five miles down the road from the trailer. Ella gathered her courage and went to see her, not knowing that she was about to meet the best friend that she'd ever have outside of God.

Feeling very small and insecure, even intimidated, she walked up to the big double doors and rang the bell. She fought the urge to run away and hide again. Her confidence and self-esteem had grown less with each passing day since Johns' death. She felt like something less than a human being. She felt like she wasn't as good as everyone else. She felt ashamed and afraid. She had to force herself to put one foot in front of the other. Expecting to find someone dressed in fine cloths and jewelry, she took a deep breath and knocked on the door.

To her surprise, when the door opened there stood a woman with short brown hair, barefooted, dressed in faded jeans and a tee shirt, still chewing a bite of the sandwich that was in her hand. Ella couldn't speak for a moment. It had to be the housekeeper. The woman standing before her sure didn't look like someone who belonged in this big fancy house, yet Ella had never seen anyone that acted more at home.

The woman swallowed the bite of food that was in her mouth and said; "Hi. Would you like to come in?" Her smile made you feel welcome.

"Oh no, I just wanted to know if I could rent that old trailer back up the road. I'm very good at fixing things up, and right now I'm pretty much living out of my car." She was babbling, stumbling over her words, so she just stopped and looked at Sue. "You must think I'm a lunatic, but I'm just so desperate. I really need a place to live."

Sue frowned, and for a moment, Ella was afraid that she was going to ask her to leave, or call the cops and that she wasn't even going to consider letting her rent the trailer. Sue's emotions were very much visible and concern and compassion now showed on her face. Somehow, Ella found herself sitting at Sue's table with a sandwich and a glass of ice tea before her, and she wasn't really sure how all that had come about. It had seemed like she was sleep walking when Sue had taken her by the elbow and guided her to the table. Ella felt like crying or just jumping up and running away, but instead she just sat there, silently pleading for help. Sue looked into Ella's eyes and saw every bit of the hurt and desperation that Ella was drowning in.

"It's going to be ok." Sue's hand covered Ella's.

It wasn't just words, their souls touched. It was as if they had known each other forever. They started talking as if they had known each other all their lives. In an instant, they recognized that they were spiritual sisters, soul mates, closer than flesh and blood. It felt like family reunited. It felt kind of like coming home after she'd been away for a long time. It was the first real comfort she'd found since John died. The tears started to fall silently from her eyes. Finally, someone understood what she was going through. She had a friend.

Sue provided food for the body and the spirit, and Ella knew that the safe harbor that she had found was not in the trailer, but in the friend. She ate the sandwich and drank two glasses of tea and she moved in and started making repairs on the trailer the very next day. Soon, Sue was out there helping. They repaired it with scraps of lumber, remnants of carpet and wallpaper, and donations from Betsy and others. They replaced water pipes and windows that were broken. Ella even painted the outside and the roof. As they worked side by side, they talked and never did they run out of things to say. Ella found that she was able to laugh again. Betsy helped, but she grumbled the entire time about Ella letting Jack have their house.

Sue refused the rent money. She said that the repairs were more than enough. It looked like a different place. The physical labor had been a blessing to Ella. She had needed to stay busy to keep from thinking so much. She also needed ways to vent her anger and frustration. It felt so good to take the hammer and pound the nails into the boards. Exhaustion helped her to fall asleep at night, but it didn't stop the dreams that had gotten worse and worse since she moved into the trailer. Ella tried to stay busy every day. She figured that the grief and those awful dreams would fade with time.

She worked mostly evening hours at the restaurant. Once in awhile, she would have to work the lunch crowd, but still, she had lots of free time. Ella could never sit still for long at a time. She broke out the old sewing machine and started making dolls, stuffed animals, decorations, and all kinds of novelties. She started taking a few of them to work and doing the finishing touches by hand during the slow hours. She would sit them by the cash register when they were finished until time to go home. That's how she found out that they would sell! Soon she was making more money from her crafts than she made at the restaurant, too much to be considered just a hobby any longer. She had to fill out applications, get a license and start a small business. She started out working out of her home, but soon had to rent a place in town. Her first good paying job was making new curtains and decorations for the restaurant where she would continue to work part time for awhile. As busy as she was, she still found time to walk in the woods at least twice a week. Soon there was a well-worn path from the trailer to the river.

Fear and desperation faded and hope began to grow. Anger was still alive and well deep inside her, but she could hide it and she did begin to pray again. Sue encouraged that every chance that she got. By now, Sue knew a lot of Ella's life story and Ella knew a lot of hers. They told each other things that they couldn't even tell to their families. This was a special blessing for Ella, because Betsy was becoming more upset and Daniel was becoming more withdrawn. He came around less and less. When Betsy and Ella got together, they usually argued. Betsy blamed Ella for letting Jack have their home. Ella cried herself to sleep at night over this. She didn't know what else to do, so she added more work to her life.

She took a computer class at the vocational school. Everyone kept talking about selling stuff on the Internet and she thought that her crafts might do well there. The first day that she went to class, she wanted to sink through the floor. She almost turned around and went home. She was older than anyone else in the class and even the teacher was younger than her. Everyone called her Miss Ella and she could tell that they felt sorry for her. Some of the young men even offered to carry the computer for her when they had to move them around and create new workstations. As for the computer, well she didn't even know how to turn the thing on.

Everyone was very helpful and kind and soon accepted her in spite of her age. She gained a new respect and appreciation for the younger generation. When Ella just couldn't comprehend something that was vital, the teacher would patiently work with her, one on one, until she finally understood. The other students would also help her. It was fascinating. She learned how to go on line, create web sites, install software and hardware, and even how to make repairs. She improved her people skills.

Soon Ella was in love with the computer. She bought one for her home and started selling her crafts on line. It was amazing. She couldn't keep up with all the orders. She hired Sue to help her at the shop and she sewed, stuffed, and glued, making the products way into the night. She offered to make Sue a partner, but she refused. Sue didn't need a job; she only wanted to help her friend. Daniel and his friends also helped out at times. Ella wished that he would come around more often, not just to do the work. She really missed him. He didn't like the trailer.

Soon, money wasn't Ella's problem anymore. It was the decreased hours of sleep, the increased dreams that continued to torment her, and the growing anger and resentment that she felt towards Jack that was taking it's toll on her. Something had to be done. This resentment that she felt was ruining her life and also her daughter's. If not for Sue, it would even be affecting her business at the store. She swallowed her pride and went in search of her friend. No way was she going to let this mess ruin their friendship.

Over lunch at a quiet corner table in the restaurant where she used to work, she poured out her heart to her friend. She told her everything, even the details of the dream.

"You know, Ella, I understand how you feel about Jack and what John did to you. It was awful and I'd feel the same. What worries me is the fact that you're not sleeping and you're having all those nightmares. You've lost weight and your color is awful. Especially today, you look exhausted and deathly pale. You really need to see a doctor."

"A shrink, you mean. I'm not sure anyone can help

me." Ella emptied her third glass of tea.

"Let's try the doctor first. They can at least give you something to help you sleep."

Sue drove her to the crowded walk-in clinic the next morning. The parking lot was filled with cars and they had to park on the lot next to the clinic. The waiting room was packed. There were two receptionists behind the enclosed glass window. It didn't take long to figure out that their names were Diana and Connie. The blonde, Diana, slid a sign in sheet and a pen through the opening in the glass window for Ella to sign her name. As she did this, she was speaking into the phone. Ella heard the page go out as she watched Diana repeat the message – "Nurse line 1, -Nurse line1." While she was paging the nurse, she was typing Ella's name into the computer to pull up the insurance information. The computer printed out the information sheet and Diana slid that through the window. "Read it over and sign here if it is correct." She made an x on the line at the bottom of the page. Ella signed without correcting anything. While all this was going on, the phone rang again This time Connie answered and paged; "Nurse, line 4 – Nurse line 4." She also continued to type on her computer. Once in awhile, she paused and wrote something in her appointment book. A nurse brought a stack of papers and handed them to her, telling her to fax them to the nursing home. Connie gave the nurse a disgusting look, slapped the papers on top of a pile at the end of her keyboard, and then went back to typing.

The waiting room was so full that there was no place

to sit. Ella was thinking; "God, I don't want to be here. I have to get away." She heard Sue tell the receptionist that they would be outside for awhile and then she felt Sue take her by the elbow and guide her out the door. Ella took a deep breath. She'd see it through. She knew that she had to have some help. She wished for a glass of water.

She left the clinic with a prescription for Valium. That night, she took one and lay down on the sofa. She was so relaxed that she fell asleep without even turning the lights off. She drifted off, thinking that surely she would rest well this night.

At first, the dream was pleasant. She was walking through the woods and she could feel the gentle breeze that was blowing through the tree leaves. The leaves made a soft, rustling sound that soothed her. Rays of sunlight shown through the boughs in places, and danced on the ground, creating a beautiful pattern from the shade and sunlight. A squirrel scampered up a tree. She had traveled this path many times before and she knew that it would lead to the beautiful Buffalo River and end in an isolated spot where she would sit on the bank for hours dangling her feet in the water. The surly brown dog walked at her side, growling menacingly at anything that moved. The dog's name was Brown. It was a mutt, mixed with chow and God only knew what else. Even in the dream, Ella recognized it as the stray that she had taken in and nursed back to health. That dog had cost her a small fortune in vet bills. They said that pets took on the personality of their owners, and Ella didn't doubt it. She could really see herself in this one sometimes. Suddenly, the peaceful dream took a different turn.

The peaceful forest suddenly turned dense and scary. The dog turned and growled at Ella. Its teeth were twice their normal size. The hair was raised all over its body, not just on its back. She grabbed a branch that had fallen from a tree and hit at the dog, telling it to go home. Instead, it scampered off the side of the path and went deep into the woods and out of sight. Even though she no longer wanted to, Ella continued along the path, a sense of dread filling her soul. She wanted to turn and run, but she didn't know where to go. The path behind her was worse than the way ahead, darker, more foreboding. She was thirsty again. Her mouth and throat were dry. The backpack that she was sure she had started out with, containing her drinks, sandwiches and her book, was no longer on her back. She looked for a spring or a small branch of water that would feed into the river to drink from, but there were none. Almost against her will, her wooden legs walked on. She could smell the moist, damp atmosphere of the river now and she could hear the sound of the water flowing over the rocks, but it wasn't the same. The air was dense and mucky smelling. She could smell the stink of dead fish. The sun was shinning brighter than usual. She could feel the heat of it burning her skin, even in the shade of the trees. She looked up at the foliage and the green leaves seemed to be wilted. She looked back at the path and saw that she was at the river at last. Ella looked up at the sky, and rubbed her eyes. Was she hallucinating? She could have sworn that she saw an angel pouring something into the river. She looked back at the river and saw that it had started to turn red. It also seemed to be drying up. The banks were strewn with red mud and dead fish. She woke up screaming at the top of her lungs, but there was no one there to hear her. If she had any close neighbors, they would have called the cops. Shaking violently, she pulled the blanket tightly around her and huddled there on the end of the sofa, afraid to move or to close her eyes. She stared straight ahead, eyes not even blinking.

That's how Sue found her the next day. Ella was still shaking so badly that Sue had to hold the coffee cup to her lips to let her drink.

"Let me get you one of your nerve pills."

"No!" Ella grabbed Sue's arm as she started to rise. "I'll never take another one of those things. You can flush them down the commode." She cried for ten minutes before she could tell Sue about the dream. The dream had seemed so real.

Sue called the doctor's office and was put on hold for the nurse. When she finally got to talk to the nurse and told her about Ella's experience, the nurse just told her that vivid dreams were a side effect of Valium. She asked if it were possible that Ella had taken more than one of the pills. Sue assured her that Ella had not done that and was told that Ella could take half of the pill instead of a whole one. Disappointed, Sue hung up the phone and looked at Ella. They both knew that pills were not the answer. Sue packed a bag, put out plenty of dog food, and insisted that Ella spend the weekend at her place. After two days and nights of no dreams and being pampered by Sue, Ella started to feel like herself again. When Sue went to church on Sunday night, Ella went back home. She was feeling much better. There were no dreams that night.

Chapter 2

Monday morning, Ella awoke to feel the sun shining through the window on her skin. She took a deep breath and stretched. At the moment, it felt great to be alive. She smiled. Fall was in the air. She could feel it. The leaves were just beginning to turn and soon there would be rain, but right now, the day was just right. She made her coffee and poured milk and cereal into a bowl. Glancing out the window, she saw the dog lying by the steps. "Hey, Brown," she called through the window and the dog wagged its tail. She remembered the dog in the dream and actually shivered once before she shook it off, picked up the bag of dog food, and opened the door. She poured out the food and the dog ate hungrily: No scary teeth and hair, no growling, just a hungry dog that she couldn't remember feeding yesterday.

She patted the dog on the head and went back inside. The house was too quiet, but she refused to turn on the radio or the television. It was still too early to open the store, but she needed to be busy. She paced the length of the trailer, sipping her coffee and thinking and making plans for the store. It was time for a little change. She had been stuck in this rut for too long. She could feel fall in the air.

She started loading her creations into the car, dolls, stuffed scarecrows, denim vests with oak leaves in fall colors appliqued onto them, and other things. It was still too early to open when she got there, so she changed the window display. The things that had been in the window went to the bargain table and she made the display window into a miniature child's room. She placed giant stuffed pumpkins in each corner of the window. They were large enough that a child could sit on them and use them like a bean bag chair if they wanted to. She put a miniature bed in the center and covered it with an army green spread. She put a camouflage pillow at the head and threw a blue and white football jersey on the foot of the little bed. Propped up against the side of the bed, facing the street, she placed a scarecrow, holding a football. On the sliding panel that would close behind the bed, she placed a giant poster of a teenage boy sitting at a desk and using a computer. The rest was just curtains and hangings in fall colors. She was not going to have ghosts, vampires and skeletons in her shop this year. Real life was scary enough for her at the present. She was beginning to wonder, though, if she should try to sell a few computers along with her crafts. If Sue ever changed her mind and decided to be a partner, she knew that she would do that.

The new display was drawing attention. People had been coming in all morning. The bargain table was almost empty. She turned from the cash register as a customer walked away and Daniel caught her in huge bear hug, lifting her off the floor.

"Gran, I want my room done like that!"

"Well, if it's ok with your mom, get the decorations and curtains from the back. You will have to go buy the spread if you don't have one."

"What about the camouflage pillows?"

"We have plenty of those. You can have a couple." If he wanted the whole store, she'd probably give it to him. He really was a good kid. She hoped that he didn't try to grow up too soon and get married too young. It was hard to believe that this was his last year of grade school. He was already interested in girls and it was easy to see that they were interested in him. He would be a freshman in high school before she knew it. Betsy came in as he was headed for the door with his arms full of stuff. He grinned and she frowned. Ella thought that frown looked so out of place on her beautiful daughter.

Betsy had always been so happy before John died. She had a bouncy personality that matched her name. Her eyes were blue and her dark brown hair had natural red highlights that glinted and shined when she was in the sun. She was always smiling then, but she almost seemed like a stranger now.

"Now Daniel! If you are taking a bunch of stuff home, you are going to have to get rid of a bunch of your old things. Your room is already a big mess."

"I know, mom, I'm going to redo it. Maybe Gran will help me."

Betsy looked from one of them to the other but Ella kept quiet. She knew that look and it couldn't be good. As soon as Daniel was out the door, the words poured out.

"Mom! Have you seen what Jack has done to our house? It looks like a junkyard over there. He has the yard full of old cars and trucks. It is so muddy and there are deep ruts where the grass used to be." She walked a few steps away and whirled back to face her mother. "That's not all! There is garbage strewn all over the yard. The big window in the front room is broken and he has duck taped plastic over it! You ought to see the creepy people that he's got hanging out over there. The neighbors are all mad. They hardly speak to me anymore, except to complain about the house. Two of them called me last night. You've just got to do something."

"Bets, honey, I have tried. The lawyer said Jack has a right to be there. The house was in your father's name and he left it to Jack. I had to leave because I just can't live like that."

"Oh sure! Blame it all on Daddy! Nothing's ever your fault is it? You make it sound like he just died because he wanted to."

"No, Betsy- - -," but her daughter was already out the door.

At the end of the day when she totaled up her profits, she couldn't enjoy the fact that her business was doing great. She was very worried about her daughter and she was so angry at Jack that she wouldn't be surprised if steam started coming out her ears. The day had started out so great. She had been so happy to see Daniel. For just a few minutes, she had almost felt alive again. Most of the time, she felt like she had died when John did. There was only this shell of the person that she used to be walking around.

When she got home, the phone was ringing. As she hurried to answer it, she vowed that she would not dump all this stuff that was dragging her down on Sue today, but it wasn't Sue on the phone, it was Betsy.

"I'm sorry that I got so angry, Mom. You know that I love you."

"I love you too, Bets."

Before she got all the words out, Betsy had hung up the phone, probably crying. Ella didn't feel any better. She knew that she was too agitated to sit long enough to sew on the machine or do needle point, but she had to do something. With the little brown dog at her heels, she went into the woods at the back of the house to gather the wild grapevines and muskadine vines that she used to make wreaths. The physical effort of cutting them at the ground and pulling and tugging them from the trees felt good. As she struggled with the vines and vented her anger, she wished that she could wrap one around Jack's neck and hang him in the tree. She pictured his big head with its long nose and odd-shaped ears that were almost pointed with the vine that she was pulling on wrapped around his scrawny little neck. Donkey or Mule would have been a better name for him, for when he sneered at her, he resembled a donkey when it started to bray. Then she thought that it was an insult to donkeys and mules to compare them to her brother-in-law. The desire to see Jack hanging from the tree with a vine around his neck was so strong that when she glanced up into the trees, she thought that she did see a man hanging there, only it wasn't Jack and he was hanging by a rope, not a vine. She shook her head and blinked her eyes and when she looked again, there were only the trees and vines.

The dog lay on the dried leaves in a sunny spot dozing, unaware of Ella's frustration. When she started dragging the vines an armload at a time back to the yard, the dog made each trip with her. Tired, she sat on the steps with her elbows on her knees and her head in her hands and softly cried. She missed John. She worried about Betsy, and at least at the moment, she hated Jack. The dog whined and gently pushed her arm with its nose. With the nightmare dog of her dreams completely forgotten, Ella wrapped her arms around the dog's neck and buried her head in the soft fur and sobbed harder. When she felt better, she turned on the porch light and used the mold to make about a dozen wreaths. After that, she was calm enough to take them into the house and decorate them with the colorful cloth leaves and big bright orange ribbons so that she could put them in the store tomorrow. She made a few with purple and green bows because she really didn't like orange and she wanted to hang one on the door of her shop. Exhaustion overwhelmed her. All her energy was drained. Her eyes were strained and red from crying. She needed to unwind. She dragged herself inside and locked the door.

Ella ran the tub full of water as hot as she could stand it then sat and soaked her body until the water turned cold. With her long, straight black hair bound up turban style in a worn pink towel, she donned her old flannel gown and robe and lay on the sofa to rest. She stretched her feet and wiggled her toes. Her skin was withered from the water, but she didn't bother to apply lotion. She knew that she was letting herself go, but she couldn't make herself care. The next thing that she knew, it was morning. The dog was barking and she realized that it was the barking that had awakened her. She also remembered that she had been dreaming about the dog, but it was just a dream, not a nightmare. She looked out the window to see what was upsetting Brown, and saw a man walking away at the end of her driveway. All she could see was his back but even that made her feel uneasy. There seemed to be a dark shadow around him, even though the sun was shining brightly. He just kind of walked out of sight; just sort of blended into the atmosphere. The closest neighbor was miles away. She listened for a car to start, but didn't hear one. She rubbed her eyes and wondered if she was dreaming again. The dog stopped barking and came to rub against her leg. She reached down and petted it and knew that she was awake. An even more scary thought crossed her mind. She feared for her sanity. Was she hallucinating? No, Brown wouldn't have barked if that were the case.

She needed her coffee. Why was she always so thirsty? Sue had wondered if she might have diabetes, but all her lab tests had been normal. She willed herself not to worry about it. She almost convinced herself that it was only a hunter that had lost his way. She decided to keep this to herself and not tell anyone. She really feared for her sanity more and more with each passing day. With every ounce of determination that she possessed, she pulled herself together. At work, she made an extra effort to be friendly and to smile. She invited Betsy to lunch. It was ok until they ordered dessert, then Betsy brought up the subject of Jack.

"Mom, won't you please do something? Jack has made an awful eyesore out our home. It hurts so bad to see it. Just drive by there and look. It's awful."

"Honey, I don't know what I can do. The house belongs to Jack and there is no way on earth that I can live there with them. June is just as bad as Jack is and those kids are downright mean. If I moved back in the house with them, they wouldn't change. They'd do worse just to torment me. You know that Jack has always resented me."

"Mom! Don't be ridiculous! I don't want you to live with them. Can't you just make them move?"

"I doubt it, but I do have some money now. I'll talk to the lawyer again." She thought for a moment, then said; "Bets, you know how much your father loved Jack. He probably did want him to have the house, but we'll see what we can do."

"Yes! Thank you! Come on, Mom, I just want you to see for yourself what it looks like."

Betsy all but dragged Ella to her car and they drove slowly by their old home. It was every bit as awful as Betsy had described it. The neighbors on both sides had put up a privacy fence, but still, it was ugly. The front yard looked like a junkyard. Shingles were barely hanging on the roof. Windows were broken and glass was still lying on the ground. You could see the plastic taped in place with the duct tape from the road. There was a big mud hole in the yard and the two younger boys were splashing muddy water on each other. Ella took the rest of the day off and she and Betsy went to see the lawyer.

Mr. Smithers met them in the empty waiting area and shook hands with them both: Still, he didn't seem too happy to see them. They followed him back to his office and sat in the two chairs in front of his desk, while he distanced himself by taking the bigger chair that was located behind it. He reared back and placed his thumb on his chin.

"What brings you ladies here today?" He looked first at Ella, then at Betsy.

"You told me awhile back, that if I had some money, maybe we could fight the will that John made, leaving our house to his brother, Jack." Ella took a deep breath. "I have a business now, and it's doing well. What Jack has done to our home is really upsetting. People who used to be our friends hardly speak to us now. This is really hurting Betsy. What do you think we should do about it?"

"Well now, Ella, you know that I was John's friend as well as the family lawyer. You know that you can move back into the house with Jack and his family at any time. John did it that way so that you would always have someone to take care of you. He was always worried about him being older than you were. He often wondered what would happen to you if he weren't around. Jack was just in here the other day and he is also concerned about you. I think it would be better if you just went back home and let Jack help you. Betsy here, and her husband are young. They can't be expected to keep you up - - -."

"Are you crazy?" Betsy was on her feet as she interrupted the lawyer. "Have you even been to the house since daddy died? Do you think my mom could live in filth like that? I'm sure that Jack is only concerned about how he can get his hands on what little that she has now."

"Now Betsy, honey, I know you're upset, but I'm trying to help." The lawyer reached out his hand toward her.

Betsy was furious. The lawyer was condescending, and Ella was thinking 'Thank God! She finally sees what I'm up against! She sat there not knowing what to say or do next. Betsy, however, was just getting started.

"How dare you treat my mom like something less than human and uphold that scum Jack! Mom and Dad worked all their lives to get what they had. They bought that old farm from my grandparents. It wasn't given to them. You know that they sold that to buy the house in town. You drew up the papers. Jack is a lazy, good for nothing bum, living off other people. He is not fit to take care of a pig!"

Ella pictured Jack taking care of a pig and felt sorry for the pig.

Mr. Smithers tried again. "Now, Betsy, I know how much you love your mother, but you know that it was your daddy that worked and kept things going and provided for you. He took very good care of you and your mother. He was an excellent provider. Why, - -."

Betsy's eyes danced as she leaned over the desk with her hands on her hips. "You sick old man! Do you think that we didn't contribute anything to the family? Do you not know that my mom made all my cloths, even my prom dress? She sewed my wedding dress and all the bride's maid dresses for God's sake! She cooked all the meals from scratch and packed all my school lunches. She kept up the yard and grew the garden and she did all that by herself until I got old enough to help her! When daddy didn't know where to turn or what to do next, it was mom who came up with the answers. She lived her life just to please him. She even quit going to church because that's what he wanted. She prepared and catered meals for his business meetings. I can remember several times when we brought food to this very office."

Mr. Smithers' face was turning red and his lips were tight. Ella reached over and touched Betsy's arm. Betsy sat and everyone calmed down. Ella spoke in a soft voice, because she knew that was her best chance of getting the lawyer to listen to what she had to say.

"Mr. Smithers, we know that in his own way, John loved us very much and we loved him. But don't you see? Betsy is his only child. You can't look into her eyes and not see a little of John. She is the rightful heir of what John and I had. Jack is only his brother and he is a grown man who should provide for himself. Surely you can do something."

"John's will shouldn't be broken, Ella. It's what he wanted. That farm belonged to his family and he sold it to buy the house in town. His parents knew that he would share everything with Jack. You might get some fancy lawyer from somewhere else to do it, in fact you most likely could, but I won't. You can still live in the house. You can do so until you die. It's not like he left you homeless. He loved you but he loved his brother to, and he didn't leave Betsy out. She got that money and she has a husband to take care of her. I'm just a backwoods, country lawyer but John was my friend. I won't go against his wishes. I just won't do it."

It was useless. Ella had known it all along and now Betsy did too. "I don't want the life time dowry." She looked the man in the eye. "What can I do about that? I don't want to be connected to Jack in anyway."

"Well, you could give the dowry to someone else… Betsy, maybe, or Daniel, but Ella, you need to think about this." He rested his elbow on the desk and propped his chin between his thumb and forefinger.

Betsy looked horrified. "No way!"

Ella thought for a moment, then asked, "Can I give it to Bengie?"

Bengie was Jack's oldest and meanest child. That kid could be a monster. At age seventeen, he already drank alcohol and smoked cigarettes. Ella had no idea how he managed to get that stuff. He was big for his age, already taller than Jack and muscled. She knew that he and Jack fought often and even exchanged blows now and then. Sometimes Bengie won the fights. Once he had gotten expelled from school, but he still managed to pass and would graduate in the spring soon after he turned eighteen. Jack had told everyone who would listen that he was kicking Bengie out the moment that he turned eighteen. He had been in trouble with the law, but his records would be sealed when he turned eighteen if he didn't get into any more trouble. Thank God that the lawyer didn't know about all that. Ella glanced at her daughter and watched as her facial expression changed from shock and disbelief to understanding of what her mother was really doing. Betsy smiled and then laughed out loud. Ella gently kicked her on the leg and some how managed to keep a serious expression on her own face.

"Well sure, I see no reason why you can't do that, but are you sure? Those kids will get the place anyway when

Jack and June are gone." The lawyer looked puzzled.

"Yes, I'm very sure. Let's get it done and get my name off of anything that is connected to Jack."

"Betsy?" Mr. Smithers looked from one to the other of them.

"Oh it's fine with me. After all, my mother is of sound mind and knows what she's doing." It was hard for Betsy not to laugh.

"There will be a fee...."

"That's fine. Just fix it up and I'll pay your receptionist on the way out."

They started giggling as soon as they got out the door. They had fits of giggling all the way back to Ella's car. The shop would remain closed the rest of the day. Betsy was the first to speak.

"Well Mom, I didn't know you had it in you. You have paid Uncle Jack back in the best possible way. He may have our home, but he sure won't get to enjoy it. It's ready to be condemned now anyway." She high- fived her mom and they laughed again. "It feels good to be free of that eyesore. Now when people complain, I can just tell them that we don't have anything to do with it and that they will have to take it up with Jack."

It felt so good to finally be connecting with her daughter again. Ella went home with Betsy and stayed for supper. It was a wonderful family get-together. Betsy delighted in telling Daniel and Rob what her mother had done and they both agreed that it was the perfect revenge. That got Ella to thinking that the Bible said that revenge belonged to God, but she kept it to herself. Her family tried to get her to stay the night, but she refused. She didn't tell them, but she was afraid to because of the dreams. She didn't want anyone else to know about that, so she used the dog as an excuse to go home.

When she drove up to the porch, the poor dog acted like she had been gone for a month. It was already dark and Ella had not left a light on. She took out her key and headed for the door, but the dog got between her feet and the door. This was strange, for the dog almost never came inside. It looked up at her and whined. She could have sworn that it was trying to tell her something. It sounded so pitiful.

"What's wrong, girl?" Ella patted the dog's head. She put the key into the lock only to find that the door was already unlocked. That was strange. She could have sworn that she locked the door that morning. She quieted the dog and listened for a good five minutes. There was no unfamiliar noise. She looked all around the trailer and found nothing out of place. She tried the back door and found that it was still locked. The dog seemed happy now. Ella decided that Sue must have come over looking for her and forgot to lock up when she left. She opened the door, flipped on the light and headed for the phone. The dog at her heals. Oh well, it was getting a little cold. She'd let it stay in. She flopped down on the couch and called Sue, who answered on the first ring.

"Ella! Where on earth have you been? I've been trying to find you. Alan has gone on a weeklong fishing trip with his buddies and this big old house is way to quiet for me. Want to come over and stay with me, watch some old movies?"

"Oh no! I don't have the energy to get out again. I've been running around all evening. We went to the lawyer's office, then I went home with Bets and we had a real family dinner. I'm exhausted, but you could come back over here if you aren't afraid of me and my nightmares."

"I could do that, but what do you mean by back over there?"

"Well, the door was unlocked when I got home. I just thought you were looking for me No one else has a key.

"Yeah, but I just called, I didn't come over. Have you checked the place out?"

"I checked outside and the dog came in with me. Isn't that strange? She almost never comes inside and she's not usually that affectionate. The back door was still locked."

"Lay the phone down and check all the rooms. I'll hold on."

Ella did, but found nothing wrong. She told Sue that everything was all right and to come on over, but now she was very uneasy. Still, the lock was fine; she rechecked it to make sure. Nothing was missing. The dog was sleeping over near the heating vent. She turned on the television just to have the noise, and then she made a fresh pot of coffee. It would go well with the chocolate cake that she had made yesterday. They would sit up and talk half the night anyway. Ella couldn't wait to tell Sue what she had done and how wonderful it felt to be close to her daughter again and free of Jack. She jumped at the sound of the car in the driveway. It seemed that her nerves were always on edge these days. A car door slammed, gravel crunched, and Sue came through the door holding the movie out in front of her.

"You have got to see this. It is so funny." She put the video in the VCR and punched play while Ella brought the coffee and the slices of cake into the living room. They laughed about the movie and after that, they laughed about Ella and Betsy's experience and the effects that it would have on Jack. The dog ignored them and slept on.

About midnight, they dragged the mattress from the half bed into the living room and piled pillows and covers on that and the sofa. They were exhausted. Sue took the mattress and Ella took the sofa and they both dozed off to sleep.

Ella heard it first and thought that she was dreaming. It sounded kind of like someone was laughing, a continuos, high-pitched, mocking laugh. As she listened, she could tell that the laughter wasn't quite human, but it was close. It was coming from the woods behind the trailer and she could hear it getting closer and closer. The dog woke up and growled low in its throat. Ella was afraid. Her throat was dry and the fine hairs on her arms and the back of her neck stood up. For a moment, she wasn't sure if she was awake or if she were dreaming, then she sat up with the blanket wrapped around her and the dog came padding over next to her. She looked down at the mattress and saw Sue stretch, yawn, and open her eyes. No one spoke for a minute, and then Sue sat up.

"Did you hear that?" She looked at Ella with a puzzled expression, rubbing the sleep from her eyes.

The noise started again, closer this time. Ella found her voice. "It sounds like someone laughing. It's coming up the hill from the woods out back." They looked out the window, but saw nothing. Ella got the flashlight and shined it toward the sound, but still, they saw nothing. The sound kept getting closer. The dog cowered between them, but was quiet. Soon it sounded like the sound was inside the walls of the trailer and was louder at the foot of the sofa. Ella banged on the wall with her fist. There was silence for a moment then the 'laughter' started again, from a different place in the wall. It went all around the house, then sounded like it was on the porch. What ever it was, it seemed to be taunting them, laughing at them. Ella grabbed her biggest cast iron skillet, turned on the porch light and opened the door. There was nothing there! Sue was close behind her with the flashlight. The sudden silence was eerie. Sue shined the light all around the yard and under the porch, but saw nothing. They went back inside and the noise started again. It was in the yard this time. They didn't go out, instead, they sat huddled in the living room, frightened and pale. Soon they heard the thing leaving, going back down the path in the woods, the same way that it had come. Sleep was no longer possible. It wouldn't be daylight for another two hours. Ella went to the kitchen and made coffee. Sue and Brown followed.

"Maybe we should go to my house." Sue suggested.

"No, I'm getting so tired of being run out of homes."

"But Ella, whatever that thing was, I don't think that it was Jack. I don't think it was even human. You are the first person to live here in a long, long time. I've heard stories, but I didn't want to frighten you. You know that I inherited this place from my great aunt. She moved away a long time ago and we lost touch. I was her only living relative. There are reasons that I was reluctant to let you live here."

" Don't tell me now, ok, I can't stand to hear it now." Ella sank onto a kitchen chair. "I just know that I can't keep running away from everything"

Sue got them each a cup of coffee and put bread into the toaster. She scrambled some eggs and they ate in silence. By the time that day broke, they were back to normal. The dog whined at the door, wanting out, and they followed it into the yard. The sun felt good on their skin. They were ambling around the yard, making plans to go out to eat after Sue got out of church when Ella felt something squish under her foot. She jumped back and when she looked down, all the color drained from her face. There at her feet lay a dead squirrel, its head missing; just ripped from its body and completely gone, not a drop of blood anywhere around. About five feet ahead was another one, in the same condition. All the blood had been drained from the bodies. There was not one drop of blood on the ground. There was no sign of a struggle. It looked for all the world like something had just bitten the heads off and sucked all the blood from the bodies. For a moment, no one spoke. There was an eerie silence, not even the leaves on the trees moved. Sue and Ella stood looking at each other. Something was very wrong. They both knew it. They turned as one without saying a word and went back into the house, the dog following. Ella headed for the coffeepot and Sue paced the small living room.

"Ella, you can't stay here. It's not safe. This is weird. Come home with me until we can find you another place to live." Sue's voice was full of concern.

"Please don't evict me." Ella tried to turn it into a joke. She was getting a little of her nerve and her strength back. She sipped her coffee and sat on the sofa. She was also getting mad. The problem was that she didn't know who or what to be mad at. This was just not fair. Enough was enough! She had been a passive person all her life, putting others' wishes above her own, and she was tired of it. She was standing her ground. She knew that Sue wouldn't really evict her. Sue would walk through fire for almost anyone. As if to reinforce this, Sue walked over and put her arm around Ella's shoulders.

"You know I wouldn't, but Ella, this has really gotten to me. I'm going to church. You know where the spare key is. If you change your mind, just go on over to the house."

Ella hugged her. "I'll see you Monday." She walked her to the car and noticed that the air felt normal again. 'Thank God!' she thought as she went back inside. She had a lot to do. She forced her mind to think about all that. She was a grown woman, after all; She refused to go around spooked and frightened of her own shadow, or dead squirrels. With the dog at her heels, she went outside and buried them.

Chapter 3

Ella went to her computer and checked her e-mail. The orders were pouring in. She was going to have to hire some help. She couldn't continue to depend on Sue and Daniel and his friends so much. They were great, but they had their own lives to live. Oh, she would always have plenty for them to do when they wanted to do it, but she needed at least one person to work full time. Mostly, Daniel visited her at the store now, and when he did come to her home, he always brought his friends with him. Her best selling items on the net were the rag dolls and the cute little stuffed bunnies with their little puffy cheeks. Each of the bunnies had a different expression on their faces. She dressed them according to their expressions to give them personalities. The really cute ones got smocked dresses or ruffles and the sour faced ones got overalls, or business suits. Some had bonnets or bows and some had straw hats or baseball caps. Some were even dressed as babies.

This had all come about by accident, but Ella loved it. Daniel and his friends had been sitting on her living room floor clowning around and helping her stuff the bunnies and glue on the eyes, and eyelashes, etc. They got to playing around with the stuffing to create different facial expressions. Some would have pointed chins; others would have chubby cheeks. Some even seemed to be pouting. One of the kids would say, "Oh look! This one looks like so and so," and they would all giggle. Ella looked the bunnies over as she took another bowl of pop corn and another round of sodas into the room.

"Oops! We better fix the bunnies faces back." Daniel told the group.

"Oh, I don't know. I think they're kind of cute." Ella told them.

"Really?" The kids couldn't believe it. They had just been having fun.

"Yeah, I'll have to pay you guys for stuffing them and you will have to see if it's ok with your parents. You can only do it once in awhile, just to get a little spending money, ok?" She really didn't want to be in trouble or accused of using illegal child labor. They had quickly agreed. None of them were ready for a real job, but they always wanted spending money, and their parents thought that it was a great idea for them to earn part of it.

Ella had taken pictures of several different bunny

faces individually and a picture of a group of the bunnies and modified her web site to sell them. The orders had started increasing almost immediately. Now she had to hire someone to help her as soon as possible. It was the only way she could keep up with supply and demand. She would ask around about who needed work before she put an ad in the paper.

Monday morning, she got to the store early. When Sue stopped by about ten, she asked her if she knew anyone who needed a job. Sue thought that she might find someone from church, but she wasn't sure, she'd ask next Wednesday. Two ladies that had followed Sue in joined the conversation.

"Your sister-in-law could use a job. I saw her and that little boy of hers at the food bank yesterday and he was asking for everything that he saw. She kept telling him no, that they couldn't afford it. The clerk finally ended up giving him a whole sack full of stuff."

"That would never work." Ella told the one that was speaking.

"Why not?" ask the other one. "It looks like you would want to help your own family first."

Ella sighed and hesitated to answer. She didn't really want to get into this. She didn't know what to say. Her mouth hung open in shock when Sue suddenly turned and glared at the women.

"Isn't it enough that she has already given them her home? What do they want, her life's blood?" Sue threw up her hands and walked away. The women looked after her for a moment, then back at Ella. There was no choice; she had to try to explain.

"It's no secret that I don't get along with Jack and his family. John did leave our home to him when he died and I signed the life time dowry over to their oldest child. I've started over and am doing all right, but I can't help but feel that my daughter and my grandson got cheated out of their rightful inheritance. Still, it was what John wanted and we are ok with it now, but it would never do for June to work for me. No matter what you do for Jack and June, it's never enough. The restaurant where I used to work always needs help. She could try there."

"We'll tell her."

The ladies looked as if they really didn't believe any of what Ella had told them and left without buying anything. Ella figured that she had lost them as customers for good. She was surprised when they came back the next day. The store was busy because she had put out new merchandise.

There was a line at the cash register and the next person's face was hidden because her arms were so full. She piled her stuff on the counter and said; "I'm so sorry. I owe you an apology for what I said and thought yesterday. I went out to tell June about that job opening at the restaurant that you told me about, because I really did feel sorry for her. I saw a completely different person from the one at the food bank. Also, I have a few friends in that neighborhood and they told me a lot more than you did. Forgive me?"

"Sure." Ella laughed. "I've been there. You don't have to buy all this to get forgiveness."

"Grandchildren. Mostly girls. Need I say more?" They both laughed. "About that job, I might be interested, if you are a little bit flexible about work hours. You would have to teach me how to do a lot of things."

"Are you serious? If you will work for minimum wage you are hired. When do you want to start?"

"Next week. My name is Beth Jones. Don't you want references? Don't you want to know more about me before you hire me?"

"Sure, I have application forms, but I think I just found out a lot about you. I'll see you Monday about nine and employees get a discount."

Ella worked late that night and the rest of the week. She cleaned out the back room, put all the stock in the closets and set up a new sewing machine. She got a used table and made a space for stuffing the dolls and bunnies, then put another one next to it for fixing the faces and dressing them. There were workstations all around the three walls with the only empty space being in the middle of the room and at the entrance. She put a small table and chairs in the center for a break area. She would probably start Beth out using the cash register and working the front.

On Saturday, she and Sue went shopping for remnants of material and other supplies that she used to make the crafts. They took time to eat out and Ella told her all about Beth comming back and about her starting to work on Monday. As usual, they were late getting home. They had been having fun and the time had gotten away from them.

It was dark when Ella pulled into her driveway. If not for the fact that the dog had now started staying inside at night, Ella wouldn't have seen it all week. She and the dog were both loners anyway and it wasn't really a problem. That's why Ella knew that something was wrong the moment that she got home. Brown was acting strange again.

Once again, the dog was crouched up against the door. It was trying for all it was worth to tell her something. It whined and cried and put its front paw over its eyes. Ella thought that maybe it was injured and she knelt down and checked it out from head to tail. She found nothing wrong. Maybe it was just hungry or thirsty.

They had heard the laughing critter twice in the last week, but they were getting used to that. It was not so frightening now, at least not when they just stayed inside until it went away. Someone had told Ella that it was probably just a mink that had come up from the river looking for food. She really wanted to believe that, and almost did. Maybe it had come in the daytime when the dog was outside. She hoped not, because she didn't want to leave the dog inside all day. She unlocked the door and Brown almost tripped her because she was so eager to get inside. Ella went to the sink and drank three big glasses of water. Her mouth and throat were so dry. She was always thirsty for something and could never get filled. At times like this, she was still almost afraid to turn on the faucet. She couldn't forget the dream about the water turning into blood. Brown was thirsty too and she drank her bowl dry. Still, Ella knew that wasn't really her problem; She would have drank from a stream in the woods or even a mud hole if it was that simple. Ella gave the dog some more water and some dog food. She fixed herself a frozen dinner in the microwave, then sat at the table eating and watching the darkness approach. The sun cast a red glow as it sank behind the trees at the edge of what used to be the garden, but was now just a field of weeds. When she lifted her glass to drink the water, the redness reflected in it and she almost dropped the glass. She took the glass to the sink and got a can of soda from the fridge. Brown whined. They were both still edgy. As Ella sat back down, she thought that she saw a man with a bloody hatchet standing in the edge of the field. She shook her head and looked again. There was nothing there. She realized that it was now too dark to see that far anyway. Must have been her imagination playing tricks on her. She tossed the food in the garbage, double checked the doors and windows, and went to sit on the sofa. She gave up trying to watch television and said: "Come here Brown, we're going to bond." Yeah, right, two miserable creatures sitting there, seeking comfort from each other and not finding it. Finally, she drifted off to sleep on the sofa. The dog slept at her feet.

She awoke from her sleep. Something had caused her to wake up, but she didn't know what. Everything was quiet and the dog was still on the end of the sofa, because she felt it at her feet. She opened her eyes and that's when she saw it. The room was dark, but there in the center of the room, was a disembodied, life-sized head of a woman. It just floated there in mid air, in the middle of the room looking serene, a slight smile on its pale lips. The hair was white and pulled back in a bun and the eyes were a pale blue. It glowed softly like a soft white light bulb, but not as bright. It looked the way a dead person looks when they are in the casket, except for the open eyes. At first, Ella didn't feel threatened or frightened in any way. "It's not real," she told herself. "It's just my imagination." She closed her eyes, then looked again. It was still there in the same place. She got up and walked around it, went to the light switch by the door and turned on the light. When she looked back, it was still there, smiling that sad, gentle smile at her, still facing her. That's when she started screaming. Her screams woke the dog and the head vanished. Ella stood there shaking. Had it not been the middle of the night, she would have called Sue. She tried to convince herself that it was just a dream, but she knew better. It had to be some kind of omen; she didn't believe in ghosts. She thought about her dead husband. If she were going to see ghosts, surely it would be him.

She missed John. She hated being alone at times like these. She wondered if she was going crazy or having a nervous breakdown because she had lost her husband. She looked up the number for the mental health clinic and wrote it on a piece of paper, planning to call for an appointment in the morning. There would be no more sleep for her this night. She went to the sewing room and made dresses, aprons, shirts and overalls for the bunnies. She had to stay busy. By the time the sun came up, she had a box full of clothing and several bunnies ready to be stuffed. At eight o'clock, she called the mental health center for an appointment. Since it was not a crisis situation, and she wasn't a danger to herself or others, she could not be seen for about three weeks. She checked her computer for orders and was shocked to see how many she had to fill. It was a good thing that she had worked most of the night. She checked her bank accounts and was amazed that she had done so well. Aside from the costs of operating her business, she now had enough in her personal account to put down a good sized down payment on a house if she wanted to do it. She decided that she would talk that over with Betsy sometime soon, but not now. After all, it would just be more space to be alone in. Most of the time, Ella still felt like she was half-dead, but once in awhile, she felt the desire to live again. She called Sue just to hear a caring voice, then she dressed and loaded the car and went to the shop. When she got there, she wasn't really surprised to find Sue already there waiting for her. Sue could always tell when something was wrong, even if no one told her. Ella felt like just breaking down and crying on her shoulder but she tried to smile instead.

"Dreams again?" Sue handed her a take out bag and coffee from the closest drive through.

"Worse." Ella winced at the memory.

They had breakfast in the back of the store and Ella told it all, even about her appointment with mental health. Sue paled at the description of the head. For what seamed like forever, she just sat there looking at Ella and not saying a word. Ella thought that she had said too much and that now, even Sue thought that she had lost her mind. She wondered what on earth she'd do if Sue were now afraid of her.

"Sue, say something, please." Ella touched Sue's hand and found that it was cold. "What is wrong? I'm so sorry if I scared you. I promise that I'll get help."

Sue shook her head and swallowed some coffee. The color slowly seeped back into her face. "Ella, you have just described my great aunt; the one that left me that place where you are living. Actually, it just went to me because I was her next of kin. She didn't really leave it to anyone. You are going to have to get away from there. There are things that I have to tell you. I know you don't want to hear them, but you have to. My aunt moved away from there because she said the place was haunted. She moved out of state and never came back. She was a brave woman, but what ever it was that happened to her when she lived there scarred her half to death. She couldn't even talk about it."

"Sue!" Ella interrupted her friend. "I don't believe in ghosts and I know that you don't either!"

"No. I don't believe in ghosts, but Ella, there are warnings: And even worse, there are demons. Jesus protects us from them. You don't go to church now, but

I know that you still believe in Him. Ella, I've never told you, but I had a battle to fight to get to Christ. They say that my great grandmother was a witch; that she could tell fortunes and cast spells. She was a hard, mean woman. No one dared to cross her because they were afraid of her. I don't know a lot about my mothers' side of my family. You know what the Bible says about that. She had a son who could do strange things – like blow in a baby's mouth and cure the thrush. The called him a faith doctor. I don't know what I think or feel about that. He was nice and accepted in the community. His daughter could remove warts from a person without even touching them. I've met them both and they seem like normal people, but I've heard a lot more things, even stranger than that."

"Sue, why did you keep all this from me? I thought we told each other everything. I can tell that this bothers you and you've kept it all bottled up inside while I've burdened you with all my problems."

"For the same reason that you keep those night terrors of yours a secret. I was afraid of what people would think about me. My family is really strange and I was never close to any of them except my sister. Mom died when she was born and Dad was gone a lot. My husband is the only one who knows all about it and he just thinks it is silly. Sometimes I wish I could talk about it, but mostly I just try to forget about it. When I first met you, I felt a connection to you that is stronger than my connection to my sister, and you know that I love her dearly. She was never troubled by the 'curse' or the 'gift' or whatever it is.

Still, I was afraid to tell you everything, even after I knew about your dreams and I still haven't told you all of it. I haven't told you the really scary parts."

Sue still looked a little shaken. She dropped her head into her hands and that was the first time that Ella had ever seen her friend cry. It tore at her heart. She put her arms around Sue and for once, she was the strong one.

"Sue, you are the best friend that I've ever had. There is nothing that you could ever say or do that would change that. You can tell me anything."

Sue laughed and blew her nose. "No, Jesus is your best friend and He's mine too. Ella, I got saved when I was only ten years old. I hate to think what would have happened to me if I hadn't. It's scary. I was worse than mean and I could have had those 'gifts' that my ancestors had and more. I could make people do things just by willing them to. They would do something that I wanted them to do then wonder why on earth that they did it. I hung out with a rough bunch of older kids and I loved to fight and cause trouble. My own father was half-afraid of me sometimes. My grandmother wasn't, though; My dad's mother would drag me to that little old Pentecostal church with her every chance that she got. Sometimes she would down me in her living room and try to 'pray the devil out of me'. I always knew that there was something different about her and I had more respect for her than I had for all the others. She had long brown hair and she piled it high on top of her head and pinned it with hairpins. I've seen her shout until her hair would actually fall down and she'd just laugh about it. She shouted the night that I got saved and I did too. It was the best feeling. I felt as light as a feather." Sue stopped talking and seemed to be lost in her thoughts and memories. Her smile was back and her face glowed..

Ella massaged her friend's shoulders and didn't say a word. She was kind of lost in her own thoughts. Her throat was dry and she was thirsty again. She sat back down and took a sip of her coffee, but it didn't satisfy her thirst. She remembered when she got saved, and when she stopped going to church. She wished now that she had chosen her Christian walk over John. She might have lost him, but she had anyway. He was dead and now she felt so empty. When she stopped going to church to please him, she told herself that a wife was supposed to be obedient to her husband, but really she knew, somewhere deep inside, that she had made the wrong choice. She shook her head and thought of the good things in her life, Betsy, Daniel, Sue, and her business that just kept on doing better. Beth had turned out to be a wonderful employee and a new friend. No time for a pity party, Sue needed her. When she looked up, Sue was watching her over the rim of her coffee cup.

"That's only a very small part of it, Ella, are we still friends?"

"You bet! Don't even try to get rid of me. We will have to share more of our strange stories. Now that I know a little more about you, I'm not afraid that you will have me committed."

They laughed and went to the front of the store, just as Beth came in. As she opened the door, they could hear the commotion outside. Beth looked frightened and as she tried to close the door, a denim-clad leg and a man's big brown work shoe wedged it's way in between the door and the frame. The door was shoved open and Sue caught Beth to keep her from falling. Suddenly Ella stood face to face with Jack, and Bengie was right behind him and a little to his left. Jack glared at Ella with a hatred that you could feel coming from his eyes. He shook his fist at her. In spite of herself, she took a step back.

"You stupid excuse for a woman!" He bellowed. "You are going to undo the mess you've made!" He snarled, "If you think I'm letting him stay there a day past his eighteenth birthday, you are crazier than you look. It's my house and what I say goes! You had better fix this mess you've made!"

For the first time ever, Ella felt sorry for Bengie. She looked into his eyes and saw more than the bully. She saw a glimpse of a frightened child. Still, he squared his shoulders and tensed his muscles and spoke with determination.

Bengie stepped forward. "Don't do it Aunt Ella. I have no place else to go and if I don't have a home, they might revoke my parole and not seal my record. I'm trying to stay out of trouble and I can handle Dad."

Jack whirled on Bengie. "Don't call her Aunt! Your Uncle John is dead. She is no relation to you!"

Ella forgot to be afraid. "The life time dowry is his.

He can do what he wants with it. You need to be thinking about how you can help him instead of how to kick him out of his home. He might not be in so much trouble if you would be a better father to him. He's your son." She wanted to put her arms around Bengie and just hold him for a moment, but she knew better than to do it. Still, she could see that it meant something to him, that someone cared enough to speak up for him. Ella decided that she would keep her eyes open for anyway that she might have of helping him.

Jack looked like he was going to explode at any second. His face was red. He ground his teeth and balled up his fists. Ella thought that he was going to hit her, but instead, he turned and swung at his son. Bengie was expecting it, though, and he ducked just in time. Jack's fist connected with the brick wall instead. He yelled out a string of curse words so foul that everyone around gave him dirty looks. The crowd that had gathered on the sidewalk parted and two uniformed policemen came up. No one had noticed that Beth had slipped away and called 911.

"What's the trouble here, folks?" The larger of the two spoke these words as he looked from Jack to Ella. "I'd rather not have to arrest anyone for disturbing the peace."

"We are just trying to open the store. I'm not sure what Jack is doing here." Ella told them.

Sue and Beth were quick to agree. Beth told them that she was the one who called for help and how Jack had forced his way inside when she came to work. Meanwhile,

Jack had regained his self-control. He put his arm around Bengie and told him that they had better be going home. Ella noticed that his hand was swollen. They walked away and the crowd was still standing around and looking like they were in shock. Bengie was driving.

"Ok folks, let's break it up, now. Party's over." The smaller policeman shoed the crowd away. "Give us a call if you have anymore problems." He said this to Beth, then both policemen walked away, laughing. One of them mumbled something about family disputes. They spoke into the radio, got in the car, turned the sirens on and drove off.

Some of the people came back, asking questions and buying a few things. Ella decided that at least, the episode had been good for business. The worst of it was that she couldn't get Bengie out of her mind. Those kids didn't have much of a chance at making a decent life with Jack and June as parents. Why had she never seen that before? She had always just thought of the kids as extensions of Jack and June. Now she knew that it might not be true. She had seen a person caught in a trap when she looked into Bengie's eyes today. She wondered how she had managed to keep her head buried in the sand for so many years. What else had she missed? No wonder that her daughter was mad and her grandson was distant. She'd made John her whole life. She had given her entire being over to him. He was only a man, not God. She was so angry with herself. God had given her a life and she had just thrown it back in his face. She did a lot of soul searching the rest of the day. She called Betsy and they talked for an hour, then she talked to Daniel and they made plans for her to take him and as many of his friends that would fit into her car to the movies on Saturday. When she got home, the dog was waiting patiently on the porch. Ella took a long, hot bath and fell into her bed. She was asleep almost by the time her head hit the pillow. No dreams, she was just dead to the world until the next morning when the alarm clock went off.

On the way to work, she stopped and bought a paper to check the real estate section. At lunch, she looked at several houses. She decided on one that had just been built on the outskirts of town, the opposite end of where she used to live, and before she could change her mind, she made the down payment and started the paper work to buy it. She consulted with no one, not even Sue. She was a little nervous and edgy, until she checked the orders on the web site and wondered if she would have to hire more help to fill them. If this kept up, she could pay for the house and have money left over in a year or two. She sailed through the day happy and cheerful, thinking about the new house sitting on a two-acre lot that would soon be hers. She liked the fact that no one had ever lived there before. She'd have a fresh start and plenty of room; maybe Betsy and Daniel would come over more often. She knew that they didn't like the trailer. Daniel said that it was creepy. Ella went home, happily humming a tune, and to her surprise, Brown came to meet her acting like a real dog and wagging her tail.

Chapter 4

The days and weeks passed by with nothing drastic happening until finally it was time for her mental health appointment. Ella thought about not going. Oh, she'd had a few nightmares, and had been awakened at night a few times by eerie sounds that made her cringe and the hairs on Brown's back stand up, but she was eating and getting some sleep and she wasn't jumping at every sound and shadow these days. She got dressed and looked out the back door. It was a beautiful day, and the sun was just coming up, shinning brightly over the green treetops. She looked over toward the old garden, and froze. There stood a man, dressed in bloody overalls, holding a bloody hatchet, with a leering grin that chilled her to the bone. He was motioning for Ella to come to him. Ella screamed, and right before her eyes, he disappeared.

Shaking all over like someone with hard chills, she knew that she'd keep that appointment with mental health. She grabbed her purse, locked the doors, and taking the dog with her, she drove to the mental health center.

When she arrived at the center, Ella left the glass down a little so that the dog could have fresh air. It was not very hot and she knew that the dog would not dehydrate. She locked the car so that no one could let Brown out or be in danger of getting bit. You just never knew what kind of mood Brown would be in when she met new people. She would only be inside for and hour, and then she would get a leash and collar for Brown. It looked like the dog would be her constant companion from now on. She couldn't leave her alone to whatever it was that was spooking both dog and owner day in and day out.

The first part of the visit was used up filling out insurance forms and taking tests. After that, she saw the nurse, who took down her life's story and asked her tons of questions. Then she briefly met the doctor, who said that he would review the information and see her in a week. Ella left disappointed. She had wanted and needed answers and she still had none. Still, she knew that it would take time, and she would keep the appointment next week. She bought all the things that she needed and took the dog to work with her. That didn't work very well, because Brown kept barking at the customers. At noon, Ella took her back home and left her inside for the rest of the day. Everything looked ok, no bad vibes in the air, Ella was tempted to take the rest of the day off and rest, but she couldn't do that. She was barely keeping up with all the orders now and at times she even worked on Sunday. Still, she couldn't make herself go back to the store. She would just work at home.

Ella could feel herself withdrawing from people and life more and more each day. To cover it up, she used work as an excuse. She put dark curtains and shades over all the windows in the trailer, even the ones in the door. She let Beth open the store and told her to call Sue if she needed anything. Ella sewed non-stop in her little sewing area at home all day and way into the night. Finally, she was so exhausted that she fell asleep while cutting out a new bonnet for a bunny. She didn't even realize it when she dropped the scissors on the floor. She awoke after two hours, went to the bathroom and washed her face and went back to working. When she was busy, she didn't think as much. She didn't want to think, or sleep, or dream. She heard her stomach growl, but she didn't feel hungry. She didn't want to cook food, and she especially didn't want to turn on the faucet. She would rather just be thirsty. That was a normal feeling for her by now anyway. She couldn't think of water without thinking of blood. She just kept on working and piling the stuff on the floor by the machine. The phone rang a few times and she heard it, but didn't answer it. Inside the trailer, with the lights on, she couldn't tell if it was day or night. She heard a car pull into the drive, and someone knocked on the door. Brown barked and after about five minutes, whoever it was went away. Ella kept on sewing.

She had dozed off again. The dog woke her up, standing near her face whining. She pushed herself up, and to her surprise, felt very weak. Her mouth and throat were so dry. She couldn't tell how long it had been since she had eaten. The dog must be hungry too. She dragged herself to the kitchen and gave it food and water, then she got a glass of water for herself. She remembered letting the dog in and out a few times, but she didn't remember feeding it. The water filled her up and she no longer felt hungry. She boxed up all the clothing that she had made and lay the bunnies that were ready to be stuffed aside and then she lay on the sofa to rest for awhile. Soon she drifted off to sleep. She was only half awake when she heard the car in the drive and then someone knock on the door. She didn't get up, just started to go back to sleep. She thought she heard a key turn in the door, but she wasn't sure that she wasn't dreaming, until the door opened and Sue came rushing in.

"What on earth is going on with you? I've been so worried. No one has seen you in over two days. Ella! Is it the dreams again?" Sue was kneeling by the sofa gently shaking her, concern showing on her face.

Ella woke up all the way and sat up. "I've just been working and I guess I lost all track of time. What day is it anyway?"

Sue looked even more concerned. "It's Thursday and no one has herd from you since Monday. That's when you had the appointment with mental health. How'd that go?"

"Ok, I guess. I mostly filled out forms and answered questions. Took some really weird tests. The nurse took down my life's story, and the doctor said he'd see me next week. I didn't get any answers yet. I was a little disappointed but I guess I'll go back Monday." Ella got up and headed for the kitchen. "Want some coffee?"

"No thanks, it's almost bedtime, but when was the last time that you ate?"

"Monday, I guess. I'm a little hungry, what about you?"

"No, I ate an hour ago. You better eat now. You've lost weight again. After you eat, you can tell me what's with the dark curtains and why you and the dog are barricaded in here like this. I know that it wasn't just the doctor visit." Sue sat back and waited.

"No." Ella poured a glass of milk and made a peanut butter sandwich. "It started before that. I woke up Monday morning and thought about canceling the appointment. I'd been doing so much better. I opened the back door and looked out toward the old garden. I saw a really scary looking man standing there. He had on old bloody overalls and he was holding a bloody hatchet and he was motioning for me to come there. Then right before my eyes, he just vanished. I took the dog with me to the doctor and to work because I couldn't leave her here alone, but that didn't work out very well. When I brought her home at noon, I just couldn't face anything or anyone. I started sewing, you know, just to stay busy and to keep from thinking. I sure hope that sales don't drop off because I've made a ton of stuff.

Sue had turned pale. "Ella, you have got to get away from here. This place is evil. I remember now why I lost contact with my aunt. I was afraid to come here and she was afraid to step foot outside this trailer. You can stay with me or we can find a nice place for you to rent. I'll help you move."

"Oh no! I didn't tell you that I'm buying a house. I've put up the down payment and started the paper work. I should be able to move into it in a few weeks, but Sue, do you really think a place can be evil?"

"Well, I don't know, there must be reasons that people say that places are haunted. You know in the Bible, when Moses stood on the mountain of God, He told him to take off his shoes because he was standing on Holy ground. That may have just been because he was in the presence of God, but if ground can be holy, maybe it can be evil. Think about it. Did you have these awful dreams and hallucinations before you moved here?"

"Well no, but all that was right after John died and Jack moved into our house, and I was living in my car. Betsy was mad at me. I was barely sleeping enough to dream until I moved in here. I used to have prophetic dreams, you know, the kind that come true, and I've had a few visions in my life, but this stuff is different. Sometimes I think I've really gone crazy."

Sue shook her head. "I don't think so. You've worked a miracle with your finances and that little shop. I've never seen a business do so well. You started out with nothing and look at you now."

"Yeah, but you still won't be my partner." Ella laughed. "You're right though, about business doing well. In about two years, if the business keeps on doing this well, I can have my new house paid for."

"About business, Beth tried to call you. She can't keep up with all the orders. I worked up front today and she processed orders. The stock at the store is almost depleted and all the mail orders are still not filled. She up-dated everything on the computer in case you wanted to check it out." Sue looked worried again. "Ella, there was a man and his wife who used to live here a long time ago, before my aunt did. I had forgotten all those old stories about them. They raised pigs. She fed and cared for them, and he slaughtered and butchered them for meat. There was one that she kept for a pet, and one day he killed and butchered it. She never forgave him, and one day, he went berserk and killed her. He slaughtered her and cut her up in pieces then wrapped her in the white butcher paper that he bought in those big white roles. A few days later, they found him hanging from a tree out back. Some said that he hung himself, but others thought that an angry mob had done it because he killed his wife."

This time, Ella turned pale. She remembered the time when she had been pulling the vines and had glimpsed a man hanging in the tree. At the time, she had just thought that it was because she was so angry with Jack; now she thought that maybe it was the beginning of her hallucinations, or whatever they were.

"Please come home with me," Sue said. "You can bring that dumb dog."

Ella shook her head. "I'll be fine. Don't worry."

Still, she was very anxious when Sue left. She checked on the orders, glad that her computers at home and at the office were connected. When she saw how many orders were still unfilled, she went back to work. By morning, she had them packed labeled and ready to ship as soon as the post office opened. She stopped and mailed them on the way to the shop. Ella worked in the back again and put Beth in the front of the store, taking care of the customers. When Daniel got home from school, she called him to see if he and his friends wanted to work for a few hours. At first, she thought he was going to say no.

"Where will we be working at, Gran?"

"I thought you might come over here to the shop. It's not far and you could work for a couple of hours and still be home early. I have a lot of bunnies and dolls to stuff and dress. I'll buy pizza and coke, besides I'll pay you."

"Ok, let me call the gang and we'll be there in about thirty minutes. I'm glad we're working at the store and not at your home." He hung up, leaving Ella wondering why he preferred working at the store. She knew that he didn't come around as much these days, but she had thought that he was just growing up and becoming more independent. She shrugged it off and ordered the pizzas and cokes. Those kids could put away a lot of food. She would let them work for a couple of hours before they ate.

The store came alive with laughter and jokes as the kids burst through the front door. Beth jumped back and pretended to be horrified.

"Ella! Help! We're being mobbed!" She ran behind the cash register.

The kids loved it. They circled around her, laughing. "Let's put Mrs. Beth in the display window!" one of them suggested.

"Yeah!" The others quickly agreed.

Ella went to the rescue. "I thought you guys came to work."

"Party Pooper." Daniel said as he kissed her cheek. "Ok guys, let's make funny bunnies, we need the money."

They went to the back and went straight to work. Ella and Beth just stood there for a moment, listening to the boys teasing each other and laughing. They closed an hour late, but once again, they were caught up and had a little extra merchandise on hand. Ella was exhausted. She drove straight home and was glad that there was still a little daylight when she got there. She let the dog in, turned on the lights, and locked the door. The dog had dry dog food and water, and she drank a glass of milk, then collapsed on the sofa. When the dog barked and whined at the back door wanting out, Ella thought her eyes were playing tricks on her. A man was at the well house with his head inside, bent over the pump. He looked familiar. Just as Ella was trying to convince herself that it wasn't real, Brown growled and took off toward the man barking with all her might. The man threw whatever it was that he had in his hand at the dog and took off running through the woods in a different direction from the path that led to the river. She could hear him tearing through the branches of the trees. The dog followed for a few minutes and then came back to the house.

Ella took the big flashlight out to the well house and checked to see if it was damaged. A pipe had been cut into and water was spewing everywhere. She cut the water off at the pump house and went inside to get a coupling and the pipe glue that was left over from when she and Sue had fixed up the place. It was easy to fix and she wondered what that man would have done if he hadn't been caught and who would want to do something like that to her. The only one she could think of was Jack. She shinned the light around and found a container of lye that she knew wasn't there before. In the yard, she found the pipe cutter that he had thrown at the dog. She took a plastic bag from the kitchen and collected the items; careful not to touch them, then she called the sheriff. She was surprised that the sheriff actually came out to her home.

She showed him the lye and the pipe cutter. With his light, you could see the big footprints around the well house and the broken branches where the man had run into the woods. Ella tried to get the sheriff to check for fingerprints, but he said that it would do no good since they had no one to compare them to. He did check around in the woods to be sure that whoever it was had gone and wasn't still lurking around.

Ella thought about asking him to talk to Jack, for

that's who she thought it was, but she knew that it would do no good. She did tell him about Jack causing trouble at the store. When the sheriff left, she let the water run in all the faucets for a few hours, just in case that man had somehow managed to get some of the lye into the pipes. She didn't see how he could have done so from the way he had cut the pipe. He must not have know what he was doing, which was just another reason that she thought that it was Jack. He had always messed things up and had to get John to fix the mess. She forced herself to think of other things, then she turned all the water off and went to bed She prayed that she would not have any dreams and was asleep as soon as her head hit the pillow. When she awoke and looked outside the next morning, it was almost noon. She was about to panic before she realized that it was Sunday.

Brown kept going to the kitchen, then to the bedroom, and back to the kitchen.

"Oh, come on, you can't be starving." Ella said to the dog. She poured it a bowl of dog food and it looked disappointed. "Ok, I guess you can have a biscuit and egg and bacon too." Ella started cooking the breakfast and Brown perked right up. She had a fleeting thought that it was a good thing that she had that appointment tomorrow. Talking to a dog couldn't be all that normal. Still, she felt good.

After breakfast, she dressed in her jeans and tee shirt and sneakers. She filled the backpack with colas and snacks, a small blanket and a book. She realized that she had been avoiding the woods and the river. She knew that this was silly. She had always loved nature and solitude. Somewhere deep inside, she wanted her life back. She wanted to smile and laugh; she wanted to feel the sunshine on her shoulders and wind blowing on her skin and today, she was going to do so. She thought about removing the dark coverings from the windows, but she wasn't quite that brave yet. She shouldered the backpack and headed for the door.

"Want to go, Brown?" She could have sworn that dog nodded its head.

They were at the river in no time. Ella spread the blanket and sat on the banks, watching the emerald green water flow by. Brown looked hopefully at the backpack, but when Ella used it for a pillow instead of opening it, she scampered off into the woods. Once in a while, a canoe would float by. Absorbed in her book, Ella was suddenly startled by yelling and a few curse words. She looked up and saw that a canoe had tipped over as it rounded the bend and the currant of the river changed. They must have been new to this part of the river. Still, they were experienced, for they worked frantically for awhile and finally righted the canoe, then one by one, they were inside again. Now the yelling and curses were laughter and backslapping. As they floated by, one of them yelled, "Sorry, lady" and they were gone.

Ella realized that it was getting late. The sun was low in the west, just barely above the trees, and she was hungry and very thirsty. She opened the backpack and the dog came running from the woods. They ate the sandwiches and snacks, and Ella drank two colas. Brown looked at the can and whined.

"You're kidding! You can't want cola. Dogs don't drink that." The dog looked at the can and whined again. Ella poured some into the empty sandwich container and was amazed to see the dog lap it up. She gave it the rest of the cola and gathered up the stuff and they headed home. It was getting dark when they cleared the trees and the trailer came into view. They were both a little spooked, Ella was thinking about the 'Critter' and the headless squirrels and she believed that Brown was doing the same. They both kept looking behind them, and they were almost running by the time that they reached the door. Once inside, Ella bathed the dog, then she took a long, hot bath. She didn't like being so jittery and told herself that she was glad she was seeing the doctor in the morning. She was just about asleep when she had the hallucination. She knew that it was a hallucination, because the man came into the room through the wall, stood there and looked at her for a second, then he turned and left the same way. She was so tired that she just turned over and went to sleep. Briefly her mind registered the fact that this hallucination or premonition or what ever it was, wasn't even scary, in fact, it was kind of comforting, like someone was checking on her. She dreamed a peaceful dream about a lush, green field full of snowy white lambs. She could see them, but she couldn't get to them. Something was holding her back. She couldn't see the shepherd, but she knew that he was there. She awoke the next morning feeling that she should know what that dream meant. When it suddenly dawned on her that she did, she knew without a doubt that it wasn't a shrink that she should be seeking, but the Lord. Still, she got dressed and kept her appointment. All the way to the mental health center, she remembered her dream, and she also remembered Mathew 18:12, where it talked about the fact that if a man had a hundred sheep and one was lost, he would leave the ninety and nine and go after the one that was lost. It gave her hope and comfort.

This time, the visit went better. The nurse took her vital signs and showed her into the room. She asked her about the past week. She managed somehow to ask the questions without seaming to, and Ella opened up and talked freely to her. The doctor listened with genuine interest and the hour was over before she knew it. At the end of the visit, he tried to give her some answers.

"I'll be honest with you, Ella, when I reviewed your case, and heard you talking about dreams and hallucinations last week, I thought that it might be Schizophrenia, but you don't really fit that diagnosis. You don't seem to have any of the break with reality that goes along with Schizophrenia bad enough to cause hallucinations. It's not drug induced, your labs were clean. I know that your husband recently died and you've had a lot of family problems among the loss and grief to deal with." He noticed Ella shaking her head and looking kind of hopeless, so he held up his hand and then continued.

"Now, I'm not brushing you off. I just think that it may be some type of Neuroses, brought on by all that you've been through and I also think that you are suffering from depression. I can prescribe you an antidepressant. If you feel that this helps, we'll be glad to keep seeing you and help you work through it. I know that it's going to take some time, but I don't see any need for hospitalization. You seem to be functioning well enough. You don't seem to be a threat to yourself or others. Like I said, you do have some symptoms of depression. Now that guy, Jack, he has some issues."

When the receptionist asked if she wanted to make an appointment for next week, Ella told her that she would have to think about it. "By the way, how does the doctor know so much about Jack?"

"Oh. Well, he's not a patient so I guess I can tell you. He called out here and demanded to know what was going on with you. I had him on the speakerphone, because no one else was around but us and I was typing at the time. I told him that we couldn't give out information due to confidentiality. That really set him off and he went into a rage. I was going to hang up on him, but the doctor had just reviewed your file and he motioned for me to let him talk. We know a little of what you are having to deal with. Give us a call if you want to come again."

"Thanks." It helped Ella tremendously just to know that some one else knew a little of what was happening to her and to know that everyone didn't treat her like Mr. Smithers had. She was even more glad to know that they didn't tell him anything. She actually smiled as she drove to work. She called the bank to check on the progress of her loan and see when she might be able to start moving into her new home. That's how she found out that Jack was trying to interfere with other aspects of her life, not just her mental status.

"I'm sorry, Ella, there was a delay in processing the loan, but we have it all straightened out now and will try to get it all done in the next two or three weeks." The loan officer sounded a little vague.

"What kind of delay?" Ella wanted details.

"Well, your brother-in-law came in and said that we needed to talk to him and to Mr. Smithers before we processed the loan. He provided a lot of information that proved to be false, but we had to check it out." He paused. "He was very convincing, I hope you understand."

Ella understood all right. Jack was stirring up trouble every way that he could. First by coming to the shop and making a scene, then calling her shrink, of all things, cutting her water pipe, and now trying to mess with her finances. She managed not to loose her temper, but it wasn't easy and she was determined to let the bank know that she managed her own affairs, business and otherwise.

"Look, you have no business discussing my affairs with Jack or anyone else. I have a right to my privacy. All my other accounts are there, my savings, checking, and business. That's why I came to you for the loan on the house. Mine is the only name on any of those accounts, however, if you feel the need to discus them with Jack or with Mr. Smithers, I can move them to another bank." She paused, then decided she'd said enough.

"Oh no, mam, we don't want you to do that. We appreciate your business and we will have everything completed in a few weeks. It's just that your brother-in-law seemed so concerned and then he mentioned the lawyer. We felt that we had to check it out. I promise that it won't happen again." He really did sound sorry.

"Ok, but please make a note for my file that Mr. Smithers is not my lawyer and that Jack has nothing to do with any of my affairs. My heirs are my daughter and my grandson. I'm sorry that Jack keeps trying to but into my business, but I am competent and able to manage my own life. When the time comes that I'm not, my daughter or my grandson will do it for me."

It took about thirty minutes, but they hung up on good terms and Ella really felt that the problem at the bank, at least, was solved. She realized that she was looking forward to moving out of that trailer and into her own home. She didn't have much time for long walks in the woods anymore. Free time was a true luxury these days. When she came out of the back, she discovered that Beth was swamped. Ella started at the cash register, while Beth assisted the customers. Things had slowed down by one when Sue showed up with lunch. Ella put the 'BACK IN 1 HOUR' sign on the door and they went to the back to eat. While they ate, Ella told the others about all the things that happened. They both looked upset.

"What on earth is wrong with that man? There must be something that you can do to make him leave you alone. Maybe you should get a gun." Sue thought about the dreams and things and said, "Well, maybe not, but there must be some way to pay him back." Sue had never talked this way before. She was more of a forget and forgive type of person.

"Did you call the police?" Beth ventured. "Surely they can do something."

"Yes, the night that he cut the water pipe, but they said that they couldn't prove anything. They drove up and down the road a few times. I doubt that they even questioned Jack." Ella sighed and once again, the thought ran through her head that vengeance belonged to God. The thought was so strong that she almost said it out loud. They had finished the food, but the hour wasn't up yet, and no one seemed to know what to say, so they just sat there in peaceful silence for awhile. Ella kicked off her shoes, folded her feet underneath her and sat on them. Sue moved near the door and leaned her chair back against the wall until it looked like it was going to fall, and Beth propped her elbows on the table and rested her head in her hands. They were all thinking their own thoughts.

Suddenly, the silence was shattered by someone yelling and banging loudly on the front door. They all jumped up and ran to the door, but all they could really see were two big fists banging on the tinted glass. Ella thought that the glass was going to shatter before she got the door open. She turned the lock, then jumped out of the way as Jack shoved his way inside.

"You've done it now!" Having that cop come out to my house and snoop around because of a broken water pipe! And just what did you tell the people at the bank? They won't even talk to me now. Neither will that shrink of yours! Well, guess what, you pathetic old woman! It backfired. I thought about it all night long and I'm going to tell them that Benjie cut your pipes. See how much the life time dowry helps when he's in prison! I still owe you for that little trick! I'm going there now. I ought to beat you into a pulp. I always told John that you were nothing but trouble. I tried to get him to leave you, and so did Maddie, but no, he had to take care of his 'family.'" He kicked Ella on the leg and turned and walked away.

Ella hopped around on one foot for a minute, then went to the telephone. She dialed city hall. She identified herself and reminded them of the night that her pipe was cut. "Jack says that Benjie cut it." She told the person on the phone. "I've decided that I just want to let it go, since it's all in the family and everything. I'm sure he was just upset about something. I'm sure it won't happen again."

"Oh wait, Ella, Jack just walked in." She paused and then spoke to Jack. "Jack, I can save you some trouble. Ella is on the phone and she says just to forget the pipe incident. She says it's just a family matter. She is not going to press any charges."

Over the phone, Ella heard Jack utter a curse word and then she heard a door slam. She imagined that steam was coming out his ears.

"Boy! He sure is upset. I wouldn't want to be Benjie tonight. Bye Ella."

"You don't know the half of it," Ella told her. "I just didn't want Benjie to be arrested. You know how teenagers can be. Thanks."

She hung up the phone and looked up to see Sue and Beth standing there looking at her with their mouths open.

"What? You know he's just trying to get Benjie in trouble and get him in jail again. He's almost eighteen now and then his juvenile records will be sealed and he can start over and get a better life. Besides, Benjie didn't do it."

"We know, Ella, it's just that - -, well, we didn't know you had it in you. That was quick thinking and very clever."

Ella looked from one of them to the other and shook her head. First Betsy had said that to her when she gave the lifetime dowry to Benjie, and now these two. Did everyone in the world see her as some kind of quiet little mouse that couldn't even squeak? She had finally accepted that John had thought of her like that, but she was not going to have everyone else seeing her that way. She straightened her shoulders and stood as tall as she could.

"Does everyone think that I'm just dull and dumb? I love you two a lot, but I do have a brain." She couldn't hold back the tears that slid silently down her cheeks."

"Of course not." They were both hugging her and talking at once. "It's just that we are not used to seeing you like that. You got him good. You go girl! We're on your side." They all laughed and then Ella took a few hours off.

She walked out of the store and down the block to the beauty shop. It wasn't very busy since it was a weekday, and Ella went inside.

"Can we help you?"

"Yes, I'd like to get my hair cut. Can you do it now?" Her hair was swinging even with the back pocket of her jeans.

"I can get you in about five minutes. Do you just want it trimmed, or do you want it shoulder length?"

"No, I want it cut short." Ella pointed to a picture on the wall. "Like that."

"Are you sure? Have you ever had it that short before?"

"I'm very sure." Ella smiled and took a seat.

An hour later, when she left the beauty shop, she looked like a different person. She bought a new supply of make up and some new perfume. She started back to the shop, then changed her mind and crossed the street to the clothing store. She found a swingy little skirt in pastel, floral colors with a little ruffle around the bottom. It came just to her knees and swung a little when she walked. She found a perky little blouse to match, and smiled when she looked into the mirror. She purchased the items and wore them out of the store, with her jeans and tee shirt in the bag. Her favorite sandals slapped the sidewalk with a new bounce and a couple of men whistled at her as she walked back to the store. When she entered the store, Beth greeted her with a friendly smile and said; "Just let me know if you need any help."

"Thanks Beth, I always do." Ella smiled and Beth shrieked.

"Sue! Come in here a minute." She called, still staring at Ella.

"What is it?" Sue emerged calmly from the back room, munching on an apple, a questioning look on her face.

Beth just pointed at Ella and Sue's smile lit up the room. "Ok, who are you and what did you do with Ella?" She paused a minute then said, "Does Betsy know?"

"No, just you two so far. Do you think she'll be upset?"

"No. You look great. You look ten years younger. Why didn't you do this years ago?" Both women were still staring. "That dumb dog will probably bite you."

Ella faked a hurt look. "Sue! I thought you liked my dog."

"Oh, I do, but you have to admit, she sure is not a normal dog." They all laughed. They closed up and headed for home. Ella didn't really want to go home. She thought about going to see a movie and then out to eat, but then she thought about the dog being left outside in the dark alone and of all the things that had happened. She couldn't do it; besides, going out alone wasn't much fun. She went through the drive through hamburger joint and got two meals, one for her and one for the dog. When she got home, the dog was delighted with the food and didn't seem to notice anything different about Ella. After they ate, they fell asleep in the living room, Ella on the sofa and the dog by the heating vent. Winter was definitely in the air.

The shrill ringing of the telephone woke Ella and she rubbed the sleep from her eyes. She looked at the clock. It was midnight and she almost panicked. All she could think of was that something must have happened to Betsy or Daniel. No one ever called her in the middle of the night. She grabbed the receiver and managed to say; "Hello?"

All she heard was the sound of a woman crying. Her fear increased. It didn't really sound like Betsy, but if something was wrong, Betsy might sound different. She spoke her daughter's name softly into the phone.

"It's not your stinking daughter!" The voice at the other end snarled. "I hope you're happy, now that you've got what you always wanted. Yes, I know that it's your fault that John is dead, and now you're causing trouble for Jack."

"Who is this?" Ella demanded. "Why are you calling me in the middle of the night? Are you drunk or something?" Ella didn't know what to think. It wasn't a wrong number, because whoever it was knew that Betsy was her daughter. Suddenly she feared for her daughter's safety. She had thought until now that Bets and Daniel were safe. Now she wasn't so sure and it made her angry.

"Who are you?" she almost screamed into the phone. The crying stopped and the woman snickered.

"Oh, don't pretend that you don't know who I am! John always thought that you were so innocent and had to be protected, but I know better! I was going to tell you about us, but you went and killed him first. Maybe you already knew and just couldn't stand for him to be happy with someone else. I tried to get him to just leave you, but no, he didn't want to hurt you." The crying started again, and the receiver slammed in her ear.

Ella sat there staring at the receiver in her hand a good five minutes before she thought to dial star 69. When she did, a recorded voice said, "We're sorry, the last number that called you line is not known. This call was received at 12:04 on…. Ella hung up the phone. Ella paced the floor in small circles, while the dog looked at her and whined softly. Was Jack getting his sick friends to help him torment her? Would he stoop so low as to harm Betsy and Daniel? In the past, he'd pretty much ignored them. She was really frightened to think that. She patted the dog on the head and tried to think. Who was it that Jack had said tried to help him convince John to leave her? Molly? Mattie? No. Maddie! That was it. Someone named Maddie had helped him try to get John to leave her. Who was she and why would she do that? Ella didn't even know anyone by that name.

She forced herself to think back, but she couldn't remember John mentioning that name. She tried to remember everything about the months before his death.

He had been a little stressed, but that was not all that unusual, and he had been assigned to a couple of new offices in his area. He always seemed glad to get home. He had held her a little tighter on the few occasions that he had overnight trips, but there weren't that many. She had never even thought that he would be unfaithful. She had worried more about the time that he spent with Jack than she had about his job. She knew that Jack wasn't faithful to June, but she wasn't faithful to him either. John had said that they stayed together for the children's sake, but Ella didn't think that either one of them really loved the kids, especially Bengie. John wouldn't have used that for an excuse, for Betsy had been grown and married for a long time. She convinced herself that this 'Maddie' was just a friend of Jacks and was just helping him to torment her. But what about the crying? And the woman really was angry. She couldn't go back to sleep, so she did what she always did and went into the sewing room to work on her crafts. She even came up with some new creations. The dog went back to sleep and the phone stayed silent.

Chapter 5

Time had somehow gotten away from her. The weeks had passed, and fall had begun to turn to winter. Thanksgiving had come and gone and Ella had spent the day with Betsy, Rob, and Daniel. They had a quiet, but happy day together. They could remember John now without crying. They could smile at the pleasant memories of the past and name several things that they were thankful for. They sat around and relaxed and just talked for hours. At the end of the day, Ella helped Betsy clean up, and then took the turkey bones home to the dog. As she drove home, she couldn't help but let her mind wonder to the past. She felt almost content at the moment. This had been a good day.

It seemed a little strange not to have to cook the turkey and fix the huge meal. She had done that ever since her first year of marriage to John. Even before Betsy was born, they had invited John's parents and Jack over for the holidays. When the parents died and Jack married June and the kids came along, the family gatherings continued. There were often other guests, some of them unexpected, but always welcome. The number of people who gathered at her house had grown larger with each passing year until it turned into an all day party. She had learned to prepare tons of food the day before and add the finishing touches on Thanksgiving morning. The men watched football, the women talked and laughed while the kids played board games, and once in awhile, had a few arguments. The house would be so full that you had to step over kids to walk through a room. Ella served the food and drinks, washed the dishes, supervised the kids, and tried to keep everyone happy, and loved every minute of it. By ten in the evening, everyone would be gone. John would comment on how great the day had been, and Ella would tumble into bed exhausted, knowing that the same thing would happen all over again in about four weeks at Christmas. No matter how tired she was, she kept her feelings to herself and didn't complain, telling herself that she did it to make John happy. She realized now that it had made her happy too and realized even more just how much she still missed him. She felt the tears run down her cheeks as she pulled into the drive and up to the porch.

It was only seven, but it was already dark. She had been lost in her memories and had not even noticed that she was home until the mailbox loomed before her. She remembered that she had left the dog out, planning to be home early. It was no where to be seen, and fear prickled the little hairs on the back of her neck. Ella rolled down the window and called. "Brown…" No answering bark or whine was heard. The dog wasn't on the porch as she normally would be and she didn't come to the car to meet her. Ella took the flashlight from the car and shined it around the yard. Nothing. It's my fault if something has happened to her, she thought. I should never have left her out after dark. Feeling worried and guilty, she put the light back in the car and grabbed her keys and purse. It was so dark. She realized that she should have kept the light, but the car was now locked and the porch was right in front of her. She had slipped the key to the door between her middle and index finger out of habit in case she needed it for a weapon, so she took a few steps toward the porch, still hoping to see the dog.

"Ella!"

The woman's voice sounded vaguely familiar, but Ella couldn't put a name to it. Ella turned and someone stepped out of the trees at the side of the trailer. She was dragging the dog by a rope that was tied around its neck and something that looked like a sock was secured around its mouth and nose. Ella looked at the dog, then back at the woman, still not sure what was happening.

"I just had to be sure that it was you," the woman snarled "What did you do with all that nasty, long hair?" She came a little closer and Ella could see the evil look in her eyes.

Ella knew that she had heard that voice before, but she still couldn't figure out who it was. The dog struggled to get away and the woman yanked the rope. She definitely wasn't a friend. Ella opened her mouth to say something, but before she could utter a word, the woman beat her to it.

"This was going to be my Thanksgiving with him! But No! You had to ruin it! You and that brat of yours had all the others and this was going to be mine. He was going to call the day before and say the car broke down. We were going to have two whole days together and you just couldn't stand it."

Ella's eyes had adjusted to the dark and she could now see better. The woman had slowly gotten a little closer, and there was a little slack in the rope that she had around the dog's neck. Ella started to hope that the dog could get away. Suddenly, the woman lifted up her right hand and lunged toward Ella. Just in time, Ella saw the knife and stepped to the side. It was pure instinct that made her trip the woman. Her foot shot out without her even thinking about it. The dog jerked loose and Ella screamed. "Run Brown!" As the woman fell, she plunged the knife into the ground and her head hit a tree root that was barely visible above the ground.

Ella had somehow dropped the keys. She had no weapon. Adrenaline surged and she quickly jumped on the woman's back and placed her knee on her spine like she had seen them do on television. She had little hope that it would work, because her adversary had a good forty pounds on her. If she'd only kept that flashlight, she could have hit her on the head. She yanked the arms behind the woman's back while she was still addled, but had little hope that she could hold her for any length of time, and no one was likely to come to the rescue. Desperately, she wished for a cell phone.

As Ella tried to think what to do next, she felt something nudge her leg. Brown! That crazy dog hadn't run! It had come to her side. The rope was still dangling from its neck, and Ella grabbed it and tied the woman's wrists together. She then untied the other end from Brown's neck and tied the ankles. Ella could tie a good knot with rope and do it quickly. She had worked on that farm for a lot of years.

Feeling a little safer now, she checked the dog. It had a sock over its mouth and nose, secured with rubber bands. Underneath that, someone had wrapped a role of gauze around it with the nostrils almost covered. Ella took it off and the dog looked at the woman who was now flopping around on the ground kind of like a fish out of water and growled. You could tell that Brown wanted to bite her.

Ella shook her head and stood up on wobbly legs. She took a deep breath and looked at the dog. "Are you sure that you are a real dog?" She asked it. Then she shuddered, because she could have sworn that the dog smiled at her.

The woman on the ground was cursing and grunting as she tried to get the knife out of the ground with her teeth. Ella didn't think that she would be able to reach the rope and cut it even if she succeeded, but she wasn't going to take that chance. She used the gauze that she had taken off the dog and pulled the knife from the ground and placed it on the porch. The knots were still secure, so Ella felt around on the ground until she found her keys and with shaking hands, unlocked the door. The dog beat her inside and went to the sink and whined.

"Yeah, me too." Ella told it as she turned on the faucet. "Let's just hope it's not blood." She filled the dog's bowl and then she drank two big glasses of water. Then she called the police. After that she called Sue. Ella and Brown sat on the porch and waited. Sue arrived in five minutes, but the police took twenty minutes to get there.

Sue's car skidded to a stop just inches away from Ella's and at an angle. The headlights shined on the woman on the ground. She shoved the gear in park, leaving the lights on and the motor running. She got out of the car and walked around and around the woman. "Oh my God! Ella! What on earth?" Calm, dependable Sue was babbling! She kept looking from Ella and Brown sitting on the porch to the cursing woman on the ground. "Who is she? Why is she tied up? Did someone dump her out here like that?"

Ella was getting hysterical. Sue was so funny. It started out as nervous laughter and now she couldn't stop it. She was shaking and her laughter sounded funny. Sue got control quickly. She went inside and got a glass of water for Ella.

"Here, drink this."

When Ella wouldn't, Sue threw it in her face. Ella

caught her breath and finally gained control. She pointed to the knife lying on the porch, and to Brown's nose, which was now a little swollen. Finally, she could speak words.

"I don't know who she is. She was here waiting in the woods for me when I got home. She had a home made muzzle on Brown and a rope around her neck. She tried to attack me with that knife and Brown got loose. I told that silly dog to run, but she didn't. When I jumped out of the way of the knife, I tripped her and she fell. She hit her head on that root and stuck the knife in the ground. I jumped on her back and put my knee in her spine to keep her down and Brown came to help me. I knew I couldn't hold her for very long, so I tied her up. I think she may be crazy. I know it's not one of those crazy dreams that I have, because I'm always helpless in them."

"That must be her car, parked on the side of the road down there. I almost hit it." Sue had one arm around Ella and one around Brown.

The woman on the ground was calmer now. She was trying to get them to let her loose. "You do know who I am. I know that you do. I'm Maddie. I talked to you on the phone, but you just blew me off. Jack said that you would do that. He told me not to talk to you, that it would just cause trouble if you knew anymore. I know that he told you that I wanted John to leave you. He told me. He would have too if you hadn't caused him to have that heart attack. Come on Ella, drop the act. You had to have known about us."

They were all quiet for a minute. Sue's mouth was open; her sympathy for the woman was now gone. The sheriff and his deputy pulled up. Ella had to repeat it all for them. Sue added that she thought it might be Maddie's car out on the side of the road, just out of sight of the trailer and one of the officers went to check on that. When he got back, he called his partner off and they talked quietly for a few minutes, then called for backup. They took pictures of everything, even the dog's mouth and nose. They impounded the car and put Maddie in jail. They took the knife, the gauze, the sock and even the rubber bands that were on the dog's nose. They questioned everyone over and over. Ella was sorry that she had gotten Sue involved. She had thought that it would be treated like it was when her water pipe was cut or when Jack caused trouble at the store. It was way past midnight when they were finally done. Sue tried to get Ella and the dog to go home with her, but they wouldn't.

"Sue, I'm so sorry that I got you into all this. I shouldn't have called you. Remember when I told you I was tired of running? I really meant it. I'm staying here until I can get into my own home. I'll start furnishing it tomorrow. The paper work finally is completed. I'll have to have a fence for Brown. If you still want to be my friend, you can pick me up on your way to church Sunday. I know that you have plans for the next two days."

"Be ready at nine-thirty." Sue yawned. "Lock the door behind me."

From the door, she looked back at Ella again. She

didn't say a word, but her eyes asked the question once more. She really wanted Ella to go home with her and not be alone. Ella just smiled and shook her head. The dog was lying on the throw rug by the heating vent. Ella flipped the porch light back on and watched until Sue was in the car and backing out of the drive, then she not only locked the door, but also checked all the other locks. She made a fresh pot of coffee and paced the floor. Why was this incident taken so seriously when all her other complaints were all but ignored? With her questions unanswered, she finally gave up and went to bed. She had forgotten about her own plans for the next few days, but now she tried to think about them.

Ella tossed and turned for hours before she finally dozed off. It seemed like each time that she was almost asleep, she would hear strange noises, or have uneasy feelings. Once, when she had dozed, she was awakened by someone speaking her name. She heard it loud and clear. It wasn't scary or anything, a voice simply said "Ella".

"What?" She actually sat up in the bed and answered before she realized that she was the only one in the room. She took a deep breath and told herself that she must have imagined it and lay back down in the bed, exhausted. Before she drifted off to sleep, she heard the voice speak her name again. This time, she didn't answer. She was so exhausted that she just turned over and went to sleep. She couldn't have been asleep for more than fifteen minutes, when she awoke because she felt the weight of someone sit down on the edge of the bed. It felt just the same as it did before when John would do that. Often she would go to bed first and be asleep when he came to bed. He would always sit on the side of the bed for a few minutes before he lay down. She would wake up, reach out her hand and feel him there and then go right back to sleep. She knew that it couldn't be John, but she felt uneasy.

She opened her eyes and saw nothing unusual in the darkened bedroom. She felt with her hand where she had felt the weight settle. Nothing was there. She told herself that the dog must have jumped on the bed, but she knew that couldn't be so. She had closed the bedroom door. She got up and turned on the light. She looked all around the room, but nothing was there. She opened the bedroom door and checked the rest of the house. The dog slept peacefully by the vent. She sat in the quiet front room and just listened for any unusual noises, but there were none. She looked out the windows. Everything seemed to be fine. The dog slept on. It must have been a dream.

The clock on the stove in the kitchen glowed a green 2:00 and she wanted to sleep. She needed to rest so that she could shop tomorrow and furnish her new house. She wanted to move in as soon as possible. She wanted everything new. New appliances, new furniture, even new curtains, rugs, and dishes. Nothing from her past was going into that house except for her family and her computers and her sewing machine. It would be a new beginning. She was going to get her life back. She was going back to church, but she couldn't quite do this on her own. Sue would help her and be a good leaning post.

Ella got up and drank a glass of milk, then went back to bed. This time, she left the bedroom door open. She thought about sleeping on the couch, but she decided that she was not going to give in to fear. She refused to jump at shadows. She remembered that Sue prayed for her every night and it comforted her.

She fell asleep making plans for the new house. It had so much room and everything was bright and new. The kitchen was a dream and it was set apart from the rest of the house. The floor was black and white checkerboard linoleum and the walls were a very pale yellow. The curtains were white and ruffled. Ella was going to have black and white appliances and a white table and chairs. She was going to put a good picture of The Last Supper on the wall above the table with a smaller set of black and white drawings of a dove in flight on either side of that. There was plenty of room for plants and other things that would be needed for decoration and color. She would do the kitchen first, then her computer and workroom. She fell asleep with a smile on her face.

In her dream, she was walking through a house. Someone was with her, but she didn't know who it was. She had no idea why she was there. The house was ok, but not one that she knew. Her companion ventured off into another room, but she kept going down a long hallway. The light kept getting dimmer and dimmer. Shadows seemed to linger on the walls and the walls seemed to be slowly closing in on her. She looked for a door, a window or any type of exit, but didn't see one. She turned to go back the way that she had come, but there was only deep blackness. It was getting hard to breathe. She heard voices, lots of them. They were just a whisper at first, but they grew louder. Finally, she could distinguish the words. It was only one word. Ella. One voice was now dominant and it didn't quite sound human. She fought and clawed at the walls that were still closing in on her. She screamed and just as she thought that she was going to be crushed by the walls, she awoke. Something had yanked the cover from her face and she took a deep breath.

Ella came awake and opened her eyes to find Brown looking at her with the cover that had been over her head, still in her teeth, whining pitifully. Her arms and legs were still entangled in the rest of the cover. Relieved to find that it was only a bad dream, Ella untangled herself and laughed nervously. She gave up on trying to sleep for the moment and got up and fixed breakfast for herself and the dog. It took forever for nine am to roll around. When it finally did, she let the dog out and headed for the stores. The dog went down the road in the other direction. Ella had a feeling that it would stay gone until she returned and she was kind of glad to know that the dog didn't stay there alone.

Ella picked out all the kitchen appliances and two new computer desks and a new sewing table. As she shopped, she continued to think about the dream from time to time. It was just a dream, but she thought that dreams were supposed to mean something. In the Old Testament, God had spoken to people in dreams. He even talked to some people that weren't really His, at least they were not living by His commandments, she reasoned. She thought about Genesis 41, where pharaoh dreamed about the kine. Ella shivered as she remembered that he had stood by the river in his dream also. She wondered if he had felt the way that she did when her dreams started out pleasant, then turned into horrors. It was possible, she guessed, because he had seen the seven fat hogs come out of the river and feed in the meadow first. That must have made him feel good, but then the seven ill favored and lean ones had come up and stood by the others. She pictured him standing there frozen in fear as he watched the seven bad hogs eat up the seven good ones. He awoke from that dream just to sleep again and dream about the seven ears of corn. The Bible said that his spirit was troubled, and Ella certainly knew what that was like. It was a wonderful story of how Joseph interpreted the dream and was exalted over Egypt and how they survived the famine.

She knew that was not the case with this dream, but still, she had a feeling that it was trying to tell her something. She had gone to sleep thinking about her new house, or at least, soon to be new house and had dreamed about an older house filled with darkness and walls closing in on her. Probably, it was just the stress from the strange and eventful day that made her dream. She just thanked God that it wasn't one of the awful and terrifying dreams like the water turning into blood one that she still hadn't gotten over. The sales personnel must have thought that she was crazy, for she was smiling one minute and frowning the next. On a whim, she stopped in a bookstore and leafed through a book about dreams. When she looked up "house" it referred to self, family, church, or the past. It offered no help and she didn't buy the book. One minute she was wishing that she knew someone that could interpret dreams, and the next she was glad that she didn't.

Ella finally made her choices and arranged payment for the appliances for her new house, but it couldn't be delivered until next Friday. She bought Chinese food to go and headed for home. The dog must have been close enough to hear the car, for she came into the yard as Ella pulled into the drive. Ella wondered where she had stayed all day. Brown sniffed the air and wagged her tail and Ella knew that she'd have to share the food. She was actually hungry, so she took a little of the food from her containers and mixed a little of her food in with dog food for the dog, and then she sat down on the sofa to eat, while she watched television. She sighed and propped her feet up on the coffee table.

The six o'clock news came on. To Ella's amazement, a picture of her home flashed on the screen. The announcer's voice continued as usual while she starred in open-mouthed surprise.

"We take you now to the small town of Hohenwald, which is about a hundred miles south of here, where an unusual arrest was made yesterday. Maddie Telley, a nurse and office manager for a clinic in Jackson was taken into custody for drug possession. She was arrested and taken into custody by the sheriff of Lewis County, in front of this modest mobile home, located about three miles out of the city limits of Hohenwald. The FBI is also involved in this ongoing investigation. It seems that they have had Miss Telly under surveillance for several months. Further details can not be released at this time due to the ongoing investigation. We should tell you, however, that the person who lives in this home was not arrested. It appears to be just the scene of the arrest. Miss Telly's car was found parked a few feet further down the road, behind these trees. Illegal drugs were found in the car."

The television showed the wrecker pulling the car out onto the road and driving away. As Ella sat there with her mouth open, the phone rang.

"Have you got the television on?" Sue sounded excited.

"Yes, I saw it. Now we know why the police acted so differently. I still can't believe that John knew people like that. I think that I'm really loosing my mind."

"I have a feeling that this isn't over yet, Ella. It's not something that you dreamed up. Do you think that Jack is involved? That Maddie person seems like someone he'd be mixed up with. Are you sure that John wasn't involved with her? I sure hope this won't cause more trouble for you."

"I'm not sure of anything anymore. Sue, I think my whole life is just one big nightmare. I'm beginning to wonder if I even knew John. I wonder if Betsy saw the news. I should probably call her and let her know what happened before she hears it from someone else."

"Yeah, I think you are right about that. I'll see you in the morning. Be sure you lock the doors. I guess you know that I pray for you every night."

"Thanks, I appreciate that." Ella hung up and then she called her daughter.

It was a good thing that she did, because Betsy had seen the news and was getting upset. Ella had no choice, so she told her everything. Betsy was furious. Thank God, she was mad at Jack this time and not her mother. She ranted and raved about Jack and his antics until she was exhausted. Finally, she said; "Mom, are you sure there is nothing for you to worry about in this?"

"I don't see how, I don't even know this woman and I don't believe that your daddy did either." Ella tried to reassure her daughter, but she wasn't really sure of anything anymore. She had planned to rest and shop and have fun over the long weekend, but it wasn't to be. She did what she usually did under the circumstances. She went to the sewing room and went to work.

Chapter 6

Sunday morning, it was raining. Ella awoke at six am to the sound of rain beating on the windows, thanked God that it was water, not blood and stumbled into the kitchen and started the coffee brewing. She had started filling the pot the night before, because she always dreaded turning on the faucet. It didn't help to tell herself that she was being silly, no matter what, that dream about the water turning into blood always stayed in the back of her mind. She thought about backing out of going to church, but she didn't want to disappoint Sue. She wanted to hibernate again. The thought of facing all those people made her so nervous that she couldn't eat. She got dressed and dug out the umbrella, and then she paced the floor. If she weren't going to church, she wouldn't have bothered with the umbrella, she would have just made a mad dash for the car, not caring if she got wet. She didn't have the heart to make the dog stay out in the rain, so when it went outside for about ten minutes and wanted back inside, she just let it back in.

She heard Sue pull into the drive and honk the horn. She felt like running out the back door, and wondered why on earth she felt that way. She used to love going to church. When she was younger, she would have been there every time the doors were open if John would have let her. She grabbed her stuff and went to the door, double-checking the lock behind her. Once in the car, she sat quietly, twisting her hands. Sue kept glancing her way as she backed the car onto the road.

"What in the world is wrong with you? More bad dreams last night? That laughing thing didn't come back again, did it?"

"No, I'm just nervous. I almost backed out of going."

"Why on earth would you do that? We go places together all the time. You're going to love it. You will fit right in, just wait and see." Sue seemed so sure of this.

It was a small church, by most standards, but Sue said that they had a good crowd today. There were about thirty people, men, women and children, gathered in front of the little white church. A few people were already gathered on the porch and in the doorway. You could hear them talking and laughing. Ella could also hear the strains of a piano and someone strumming on a guitar as soon as she approached the front of the building. They were greeted with hand shakes and hugs. A group of children called out, "Hey! Sue's here!" and came running to meet her. Ella watched as Sue pulled a small bag of candy from her purse and gave it to them, reminding them to share and not to eat it inside the church. Amidst hugs and "Thanks" and "We won't", they rushed off.

Ella had feared that she would be an outsider, but that wasn't the case. You could feel the love the minute that you stepped inside the church. All the smiles and heartfelt welcomes were real, but it wasn't just the people, and Ella knew it. God's Spirit really was alive in this place. Ella felt like crying and rejoicing at the same time, and the service hadn't even started. With great effort, she remained stoic and did neither. Sue, perceptive as usual, squeezed her shoulder and took a seat beside her. Prayers were said and songs were sung, then they divided into different groups for Sunday school classes.

The lesson was Luke 15:11, about the prodigal son. Ella knew the story well. It was about a man who had two sons and the youngest one ask his father for his part of the inheritance and went to a foreign country and wasted it. He became so desperate that he was feeding hogs for a living. He thought he was going to perish with hunger and then he remembered that his father's servants had bread to spare. Feeling unworthy to be a son, he decided to go and ask his father to make him as a hired servant, but the father welcomed him back with loving arms. The discussion became so involved and animated that they had to stop at verse 20. Ella soaked it up like a parched, sandy desert would devour water. She was thirsty again.

The time had flown by. Ella was already feeling the gentle tugging at her heartstrings and thinking that maybe God would welcome her back, but for some reason, she still resisted. By the end of the sermon, when the preacher gave the altar call, she was resisting so hard that she almost bolted and ran out of the church. She finally swallowed the lump in her dry throat and hoped the tears wouldn't fall from her eyes. Her knuckles were white on the back of the pew that she was holding onto in front of her. Nervously, she shifted her weight from one foot to the other.

The preacher said, "I really feel that God is dealing with someone here today. I want every head bowed and every eye closed. Would that person just raise your hand? By doing so, you are just saying, remember me, pray for me."

Everyone did and Ella timidly raised her hand.

"God bless that hand. God loves you. Don't ever forget that. Amen."

When the service was over, she planned on being the first one out the door, just slip out quietly and wait for Sue in the car, but that wasn't to be. It seemed like everyone there was determined to give her a hug or shake her hand and invite her back. Her emotions ran rampant. She felt so homesick, filled with longing to be back where she used to be with the Lord, back in the church that she had thought of as hers, and she also felt ashamed. She felt even more thirsty, yet she didn't want a drink of water. Her mouth was so dry, Truth be told, she even felt a little scared. Once again, she wished that she had not put her husband before the Lord. She was quiet on the way home and so was Sue. When they pulled into Ella's drive, Sue was the first one to speak.

"Do you want to go back with me tonight?"

"No, I think I'll just stay home, but thanks."

Sue certainly wasn't one to push people into things and Ella appreciated that. She just squeezed Ella's shoulder and said, "See you tomorrow." Then she just waved and drove off. Giving in to a sense of dread, Ella stood and watched the car until it was out of sight. For some reason, she felt more lonely than ever.

When she opened the door Brown rushed out in such a hurry that she almost tripped over the dog. Ella told herself that the dog just needed to go to the bathroom but still, she searched the trailer from end to end. After that, she sat down and read her Bible for two hours. Her mouth got very dry again and she went to the refrigerator and got a bottle of water. She knew it was silly, but she had a real phobia about that water faucet. She was feeling nervous and on edge again and she hated it. She thought about going for a walk in the woods, but she just couldn't do it. The realization that she was becoming more introverted each day didn't help. She used to love walking alone in the woods, even in the rain, but now she was a coward. She used to feel so close to God when she walked in the woods alone, now, she knew that she'd be jumping at every little sound. She laughed nervously as she realized she did that even when she was in the house. To prove the point, Brown scratched at the door and Ella jumped and a little scream escaped, before she went to let her in. The phone rang, and she jumped again. This had to stop. She picked up the phone.

"Hello?" Her voice was shaky.

"Mom, I've been calling you all morning. I was so worried about you." Betsy sighed with relief. "I heard that the crazy woman got out on bail."

Ella breathed a sigh of thanks. Her daughter, who had been so distant for awhile was now almost clingy. Ella didn't want her daughter to be worried, but she was very thankful that they were close once again. Just hearing her voice was like a hug that she badly needed. She had a feeling that Betsy felt the same.

"I went to church with Sue. I should have thought to tell you. I don't want you to worry, but please be careful. Maddie did mention you that night that she was arrested."

"Mom, Rob and Daniel and I drove by that church where we used to go when I was twelve. I had the strongest feeling that I needed to go back there. If I had been driving, I think I would have stopped. That was such a good time in my life. Do you think we could go back there sometime? Would you go with me?" Betsy sounded so wishful, almost like she was a child again. Ella wanted to reach through the phone line and hug her.

"Sure we can. We can do lots of things and Betsy, we can be happy again. We will have good times again. Honey, I know how much you miss your dad."

"Night Mom." Betsy hung up the phone and Ella thought that she was crying.

Monday morning, Ella loaded her car with crafts and went to work early. There was an envelope taped on the door with duct tape, and at first, she was hesitant to open it. She remembered the duct-taped window at Jack's house. It surprised her that she was finally able to think of it as Jack's house. She didn't feel any of the bitter feeling that she had lived with for so long, and that really surprised her. It felt good to be free of that, and she hoped that Betsy was also beginning to feel that way. Taking another deep breath, she took the paper from the door, opened it and read the note.

"Dear Aunt Ella,"

"Thank you for trying to help me. Dad would kill me if he knew I did this but I just had to. I will graduate in May and will get a job or join the army or something. It's hard. I won't have a class ring or senior pictures or any of that, but I don't care as long as I get my diploma and get out on my own. I just want you to know it's partly because of you that I can do it. I turn eighteen next week and Dad would have kicked me out for sure, if you had not fixed so that he can't. Thanks for everything."

"Love, Bengie"

Ella read the note again. She felt so bad, knowing that she had done that for spite and that her nephew was truly grateful. She had been so mad at Jack, that she had not even stopped to think that his children were her nephews. They'd been under her feet all their lives. Bengie could be a pest, but he had been there more than the others had, always loud, always trying to get Jack's and John's attention. That was one the reasons that Daniel was with his mom and grandmother so much. Bengie had gotten on his nerves.

Jack and June seemed to love their other children more than they loved Bengie. For the first time, she wondered why and she thought about how hard his life must be. She knew that Jack would not help him. John was no longer there to intervene, and he had intervened a lot. For the first time, she realized just how often he had done that. She vowed that she would try to help Bengie now. It would have to be done in secret, but it could be done. She rethought the duck taped windows on the house. Could that have been the only way that Bengie had of repairing them instead of Jack's way of trashing the place? Maybe she had been too judgmental. Maybe she needed to think a little more of others and a little less of herself.

She didn't unlock the store; instead, she went to the restaurant and talked to her former boss. She asked if they might have a job for Bengie. Arrangements were made for him to work evenings after school and on the weekends. He could get off the buss at the restaurant and one of his co-workers could drive him home. That way, he could get what he needed to graduate and Jack would never know that Ella had anything to do with it. She wrote all the details on a sheet of paper and headed for the school. She told the lady in the office that she needed to talk to Bengie about a family problem and had her to call him to the office, then she waited outside the door so that she could talk to him in private. He was so happy that he hugged her and she was surprised. As Bengie squeezed her so tight that she could hardly breath, she felt her heart soften a little more. She decided then and there that she would watch for other ways to help him. She felt much better when she left.

Ella opened the store, stocked the new merchandise, and greeted her customers with a real smile. When she checked the web site, she knew that she would be working most of the night. She told herself that was a good thing, because Daniel wanted a new computer for Christmas. Beth came to work at ten and Sue showed up to help at noon. Ella skipped lunch and went to the back to make crafts and fill orders.

About two o'clock, two men in suits entered the store and told Beth to close up the shop. At first, they ask Sue to leave, but when they found out that she was Ella's best friend and that she sometimes helped out at the shop, they told her to stay. They all went to the back, where Ella sat stuffing a bunny. The men flashed badges and verified that Ella was the owner.

They went to the computers first. Ella watched in amazement as one of them accessed all her records from day one. They even downloaded her files from her home computer, personal as well as business ones. Ella was fascinated that they could do all of that and that they even got her password without asking her for it. It made her want to take some more computer classes. As she watched over his shoulder with wide eyes and open mouth, the man said: "Have a seat ma'am, you can't change or hide anything now anyway."

"I wasn't. I was just watching you work. I love computers, but I wasn't aware that you could do all that. Why would I want to change it or hide it? I worked too hard to get it on there. I sure don't want to loose it. Today's work isn't even backed up."

He gave her a wry smile that said 'Yeah, right' and kept on working. He checked and double-checked everything. While he was doing this, his partner was taking inventory. With a notebook and a pen in hand, he counted every bolt of material and all the unfinished crafts, then he went into the store and counted all the merchandise. They searched the store from top to bottom, looking under each scrap and bolt. They even opened up some of the bunnies and pulled out the stuffing. The man at the computer got a call on his cell phone.

"Yeah?"

"I've checked on her business license, social security, insurance, bank accounts and income tax. Everything seems to be in order. I checked her former place of employment. They say she's honest and hard working. Neighbors say she was a stay at home wife before her husband died. I went to the lawyer's office and read that will. Man, you won't believe that one. It looks like John left her out in the cold. The daughter only got $20,000 and that was handled properly. Now the brother, that's another story, and Mad Maddie, she won't be getting out on bail this time. It seems that Dear John lived two separate lives."

"You're sure about that?" This was the one that had checked her computer. He had a know it all attitude about him. He was very handsome and wore his cloths loose. Ella wondered why she noticed. He glanced at her again.

"Oh yeah, but I don't mind digging deeper, this is kind of fun, kind of like going back in time to Mayberry or something, except that John and Jack are nothing at all like Andy and Barney."

"No, wrap it up, I didn't find anything on her either. The lady keeps good records."

Ella heard the cash register open and a few minutes later, the other man came back and handed the notebook to the guy at the computer. He compared it to what he had, then he looked at Ella and smiled.

"Want me to enter todays numbers or are you going to reopen?"

"N-no, I'm not going to reopen today." She, Beth and Sue were huddled together in the break area.

He entered the numbers, hit save, and then copied everything onto diskettes and put them into his brief case. "Sorry for the inconvenience, ma'am. You do keep good records. Looks like you are still in business" He followed the other guy out the door, whistling the theme song from the old Andy Griffin Show.

Ella, Beth and Sue watched out the window as the men got into the car and drove away. For a few minutes, no one spoke.

"Maddie and the drugs!" Sue and Beth spoke at the same time.

"John must have been involved, but I still can't believe it." Ella shook her head. "I've got to tell Betsy. There will be no way to keep her and her family out of it," She was still dialing the number when a news van pulled into a parking space in front of the shop. A man got out and pounded on the door, but they ignored him. Eventually, he drove away, but they stayed inside for another thirty minutes. Ella was the last one to leave. She sat there thinking about how upset Betsy had sounded over the phone.

Betsy was shocked and heartbroken all over again. If Ella didn't know better, she would think that her daughter was angry again. Betsy had idolized her father. Neither of them could believe that John would be involved in a mess like this. Jack would, but not John. Ella knew that this would be much harder for her daughter than it would be for her. She wished for some way to protect Betsy, but all she could do was just be sure to call her often and do whatever she could to let her daughter know that she loved her. It would be hard to keep her in the background, since Maddie loved to mouth off and she seemed to hate Betsy as much as she hated Ella. There seemed to be no solutions, and Ella finally got up and went home to barricade herself in the trailer with the dog.

Chapter 7

Ella paced the floor and Brown paced with her. She couldn't bear thinking about all her problems, yet she couldn't seem to get them off her mind. She tried thinking about her new home and wondered if she could be moved in by Christmas. It wasn't possible. The rain and cold had kept the men from building the fence for the dog. There were still some finishing touches to be done inside the house. These would have to wait because the workers wanted time off for the Holidays. There had been another delay in the paper work and the bank had been closed for the holidays. She tried making out her Christmas lists. Nothing was really working. She tried to think of ways to help and protect Betsy and Daniel. She thought about Rob, then felt guilty, for she tended to forget him. She believed that he would be there for Betsy. They had been through a rough spot in their marriage, but had seemed very close at Thanksgiving. That reminded her of the past and thoughts of Benjie crept into her mind. She tried to think of ways to help him. Thinking of others was better than dwelling on her own problems, but she seemed to have no solutions for anything. She didn't want to turn on the television, but it was too quiet. The sound of her footsteps and the dog's were getting on her nerves. It was dark already and it was only six in the evening.

Ella was used to it getting dark early in the winter months, but this felt different. The blackness was just too dense. It felt thick, almost like you could cut it with a knife. She told herself that it was just fog, just a cloud on the ground. She had seen the clouds moving in earlier on her drive home, but she tried not to feel the gloom. She used to love the rain, slept like a baby to the sound of it beating on a tin roof, even loved walking in it, but now she almost feared it. It was nearly Christmas. She realized that they might get snow instead of rain. She went to the computer and finished her shopping on line, unable to cope with the crowded malls. Resigned to the fact that she wasn't going to be in her new house by Christmas, she considered other options. No one really felt like planning a dinner. Ella called Betsy. They'd have to do something for Daniel's sake. Maybe Betsy and family should go to Ohio and spend Christmas with Rob's family. They hadn't done that in years.

Betsy had been thinking the same thing, and now she was trying to convince her mother to go with them. It would be good to get away from everything for a while. Ella finally convinced Betsy that it would be good for just the three of them to go and have some family time. She told her daughter that she would spend the Holiday with Sue, even though she had no such plans. It was decided that she would bring their gifts over on the last Friday before Christmas as soon as Daniel got home from school and they could leave early on Saturday. She tried not to think of the danger of them traveling over the Holiday season, or of not being close enough to see her family anytime she wanted.

Ella thought about closing the store for a few weeks, but decided against it. She was afraid to after that investigation. She knew that people were talking. It was a small town after all and it might look like she had something to hide if she closed up shop now. Instead, she had a sale, then worked day and night to replenish her stock. She dressed some bunnies in Santa suits and they sold very well. The bank account was still growing. She was a long way from homeless now, but she was still not happy. She found herself thinking about Bengie and his brothers, wondering if they would have Christmas. This would be their first one without John, and she was not sure if those kids would have anything without him. Often, Bengie's only present had come from his uncle. Before John died, they had spent all their Holidays with John and Ella. John had been the glue that held them all together. The two little boys were young, but still, the changes in their lives had to affect them. She was not going to try to talk to Jack nor June, so the next day she went to the restaurant and talked to Bengie. She would just have to ask him if they had any plans.

"I've bought them a few things and I have them here at the restaurant, I'm not sure how to slip them in. They are always there when Dave takes me home. I may just have to wrap them and give them to them right before Christmas."

Ella had seen an old car for sale on her way to work. It was still in good running condition. She knew the people who owned it.

"Bengie, if I get you a cheap car, could you just kind of not tell anyone how you got it?" She felt guilty about this, but she didn't want any more trouble.

"Sure, but you don't have to do that. You have already made a way for me to graduate. I never would have made it without you. Oh! I can tell you! I got an A and two B's on my last report card. Mom and Dad just think it's silly. I really think I'm going to join the marines when I graduate. Since Grandmother moved back, the boys stay over there most of the time. If not for that, I don't think I could leave them."

Bengie's boss, Ella's former boss, had been listening to every word, but no one cared. She knew all the details of their lives by now anyway. It was hard to have secrets in a town this small.

"Hey Bengie, we are kind of slow right now. If you want to leave early, you can." She winked at Ella then went back to work.

"Come on, I think we have a car to check out. Do you have a license?

Bengie grinned. "A restricted one."

Ella sighed and led the way to the car. "Bengie, you will be careful and responsible won't you?"

"Of course, Hey Aunt Ella, I've finally grown up. I guess I had to after Uncle John died. I sure do miss him."

He looked hurt and she was sorry that she had asked. Not knowing what else to do, she punched him on the arm and told him to get in the car because they had a Christmas present to buy. Bengie's eyes lit up when they stopped beside the old 91 Ford Taurus that used to be a police car. They took it for a test drive and it rode like a dream. Bengie joked about hooking the blue light back up. It was still mounted on the outside of the driver's side, but the wires had been cut off. When they got back from the test drive, Ella paid the man and they went to the courthouse and completed the deal. The insurance was a little higher than she had counted on, but the look on Bengie's face was worth it. They went to Walmart and bought toys and cloths for his brothers.

Ella found herself wondering how on earth Jack and June ever had a son like Bengie. It must have been John's influence. Still, he didn't look nor act like any of them. Remembering the way he was reared, she wondered that he had turned out as well as he had. She remembered the cruel things that Jack would spout off and how John would stop him, then look like he felt sorry for him. Once, Bengie had asked for enough money to get a hamburger and to use the car and Jack had spouted off that he guessed that since the boy got caught in his trap, he had to feed him. Without saying a word, John had handed Bengie a twenty and the keys to his truck and guided Jack out the back door. Ella had watched out the kitchen window as they had a heated discussion, but in the end, John had thrown his arm around Jacks shoulders and they had laughed. John had never told her anything about it, but she had never quite forgotten it.

That night Ella slept without dreams, but she could still feel herself withdrawing even more from everyone and everything. She just wanted to hibernate. She told herself that it was natural for her to be depressed because of the holidays, that she was just feeling sorry for herself. She was missing John, especially after her talk with Bengie. Maybe she would call mental health for another appointment after Christmas. Right now, all she wanted was to be left alone and sleep, but sleep often evaded her. Her mood was a perfect match for the cloudy winter days. She saw Betsy and family off, letting them think that she was spending the time with Sue. She waved goodbye to Sue and her husband, with Sue believing that she was going to Ohio with Betsy. She had convinced Bengie to order take out food for his family's Christmas dinner the day before. All the time that she was doing this, she knew that she was going to be alone, but didn't know why she felt such a need for secrecy. She told herself that she just didn't want to upset the people that she loved and that she just didn't want to intrude or rain on their holidays. Still, she had a feeling that something wasn't right. She could feel something bad coming on. She really didn't want to go to work. Beth wanted extra time off to be with her family. At noon on Christmas Eve, she hung the closed sign on the door of the shop with a note saying that they would reopen after New Years.

Chapter 8

Christmas came and went and Ella spent it alone, holed up in the trailer with Brown. She had started buying bottled water to drink, even though it didn't taste as good as her well water at home. She was well stocked on both that and diet sodas, none of them red. She even had some juice, also nothing red. The fridge was full and so were the cabinets. She still cringed when she had to turn the faucet on to wash dishes, clean, or take a bath. She and Brown mostly ate out of paper plates now. There was plenty of food, but Brown had to eat more dog food because Ella was cooking a lot less. She closed all the blinds and curtains and locked all the windows and doors. She only opened the front door to let the dog in and out. No one knocked on her door, and when the phone rang, she didn't answer it. She sank deeper into her gloomy little world. She found even more profound depths of despair and sank deeper and deeper into them.

She lost all sense of time. She didn't know if it was day or night, because she always left the lights on around the clock, just didn't bother to turn them off. She turned the television on and off several times, but then she couldn't stand all those special programs and all the bright, cheerful holiday advertisements wanting people to buy everything. She resented them, for reason that eluded her, never once thinking about her own ads and specials. Her sales had certainly increased right before Christmas, but she wasn't even thinking about work. She was only sewing and making stuff to keep busy, because she just couldn't sit still. She didn't want to think. She didn't want to feel. A thought crossed her mind that she wished that she was dead and she angrily banished it. She knew that she really didn't want to die. She was horrified that such a thing had entered into her mind. It crossed her mind that she was acting like a robot. She didn't even feel like a real person anymore. She turned the radio to an oldies station that played country music and just left it playing. Like the lights, she just didn't bother to turn it off. Country and gospel were her favorite types of music, but she had forgotten how sad some country music could be. It really suited her mood now. The sadder the song, the better she liked it. She and the sewing machine were keeping time to the music. It kept her from thinking and kept her from pacing. To her, it was a mindless activity, a rhythm that she got into and kind of zoned out. It was annoying to her even to have to stop and care for the dog. She didn't stop to eat, sleep, or do much else. She just wanted to stay too busy to think.

She started making odd little rag dolls with different colored yarn for hair. The eyes were buttons that were the same color as their hair. Even the clothing matched. She gave them names to match and embroidered the name on the clothing. One had sky blue hair and eyes and a shirt to match. He had overalls and blue shoes and she named him Skylard Bluie. She did the same with other colors, making boys, girls, and infants. The music kept on playing. George Jones was singing "He Stopped Loving Her Today" and Ella could really relate to that song. Tears rolled down her cheeks as she sewed black hair and black button eyes onto the white material of the doll that she was making. She embroidered the black mouth and stuffed it, then dressed it in black. It looked awful. The radio continued to play George Jones back to back. He sang "Choices" and Ella sat there with her head in her hands and cried for a minute, thinking of the choices that she had made. She picked the black thread from the doll's mouth and replaced it with red, as George half-crooned and half-cried "It's Been A Good Year For The Roses".

Like someone coming out of a trance, she looked at the doll she was holding and then looked around the trailer. Dolls were everywhere. The bed was piled full, the corner was full, and she was going to have to make some more room. Some were even piled on the sofa. The spare room was full of boxed up bunnies, wreaths, pillows, and curtains that she had done before she started the new dolls. There was one empty chair left to sit on, and Brown's corner over by the heating vent was still empty.

Ella tossed the monstrous doll that she still held in her hand over there and Brown grabbed it in her teeth and started shaking it. The dog even growled. The doll ripped and stuffing was coming out. The dog shook the doll harder, flinging the stuffing over the floor. At first Ella was mad.

"Brown! You crazy dog, put that doll down!"

The dog kept on trying to destroy the doll. It was backed into the corner with its hair on end, shaking the doll with all its might. She'd seen dogs kill snakes that way back when she lived on the farm.

As Ella sat on the only empty chair and really looked around she was amazed. Crafts were piled everywhere and her dog was having a nervous breakdown. Evidently, she'd already had hers. She started laughing and couldn't stop, and then she started crying, not hysterically, just soft, pain filled sobs. She wondered how long it had been since she had slept. She couldn't remember the last time that she had eaten or even fed the dog. The water supply, however, had really dwindled. There were only four bottles left. The diet sodas and the juices were also few in number. She opened a bottle of water for Brown and one for herself. She had no idea what day it was, and when she walked to the door to see if it was day or night, she noticed how weak she felt. The sunshine almost blinded her. She took out a couple of frozen dinners and cooked one for herself and one for the dog. She tripped over the empty dog food bag that had been ripped down the side and had to catch hold of the counter top to keep from falling. She didn't wait for the dinner to cook, she took a bottle of juice and sat at the table and drank it slowly so that it would stay down. The dog kept looking at her, but stayed about three feet away. She went to the fridge and found a wiener that looked ok and the dog almost swallowed it whole. After that it ventured a little closer and finally sat up against Ella's leg.

"I'm sorry, ok?"

The dog thumped it's tail. Ella got up and turned on the television. She had to figure out what day it was. Betsy might already be home. It would never do for her to find out about this. Ella herself thought that she might finally be ready for the loony bin, but she surely didn't want to go. What if Sue found her like this? Sue had a key and she wouldn't hesitate to use it if she thought something was wrong. Finally she learned from the TV that it was New Years Eve. Ella sighed in relief. Betsy wasn't due back until the third of January and Sue might be gone longer than that. She ate one of the dinners and the dog ate the other one, then she took a long, hot bath and got dressed. The dark circles were back under her eyes. She'd lost more weight and there was no way to hide it. Ella cleaned up the kitchen and the living room, then loaded the boxes of Bunnies and bags full of the new dolls into the car to take to the store. She made three trips and Brown went with her. After the last one, she stopped by the grocery store and barely had time to do her shopping before they closed. When they got home it was getting dark and she decided that she would do the rest tomorrow, then she checked the computer and started printing labels and postage and preparing packages to be sent off. She couldn't mail them until January 2, but she prepared them anyway. When she had her bed and a pathway to get to it cleared, she just lay down fully clothed and fell asleep. She slept until noon the next day.

She started the New Year alone, except for the dog, who was once again her best buddy. Dogs are very forgiving, she thought as she rolled out of bed and the dog appeared to be smiling as it thumped its tail. Thoughts raced through her mind as she went to the kitchen and fixed biscuits, gravy, eggs and bacon. No doubt about it, Brown was really grinning now. Ella was thinking that she only had three, four days at the most before Betsy got home and came looking for her. She had to get herself and the dog looking well fed and in good shape by then. It might be another week before Sue came home. She wondered if Bengie and his brothers had enjoyed Christmas. She thought about all the orders that she had to fill. Business had snowballed again. She wondered what she was going to do about that. More and more, she felt like a robot. Maybe she would hire someone who could sew, and someone to do the stuffing and someone else to dress them, then someone else could look them over and add the finishing touches. She could start them off at minim wage and increase their salary according to the amount of dolls they produced per hour. She realized that she was thinking about a small assembly line. Could she really start a small factory? She would have to offer insurance, some kind of benefits to all those people. Would her products still sell if they weren't homemade? This town really needed jobs. What kind of opposition would she meet? What all would that involve anyway, and what on earth made her think that she could do it?

The lawyer, Mr. Smithers, popped into her mind. She could almost hear him saying, "Why don't you just go on home and let Jack help you?" That did it. She decided then and there that she could do it if she wanted to, but did she want to? It gave her a headache just to think about it. Shouldn't there be more to life than work? Maybe she was just sick of the way her life was now or maybe she was just getting tired. Maybe adding more work wasn't the answer. It was kind of like always being thirsty, no matter how much water that she drank, she never stopped being thirsty and no matter how much she worked, something was still missing.

She wanted to be closer to her daughter and her grandson. She wanted the ache and the empty feeling to go away. She loved her family so much and Sue was the greatest friend that anyone could ever hope for. She was so much more than a friend, she was family too. Beth was also her friend, not just an employee, but something vital was still missing in her life and she knew that it wasn't just John. It dawned on her that she really might want to live again, not just exist. She was so tired of hiding, just existing, whatever. It was almost like she had died when John did, but if she were truthful, she had to admit that something was missing even back then. She finished her fourth cup of coffee and started the little pot to brewing again. Why was she always so thirsty? Lost in her thoughts, she had handed Brown both plates of food, and when she looked like she might take one back, the look on the dogs face changed her mind. She fixed herself another plate, but there was only one slice of bacon left. Ella ate like a starving person, then started loading the car and stocking the store.

By afternoon, all the dolls were gone from the trailer, and piled in the store. She was tired and thirsty, so she and Brown went to the only twenty-four hour drive through that was open on New Years to get lunch. Ella pulled into a slot and ordered two combos plus a large root beer for herself and a large coke for Brown extra, while Brown sat in the passenger seat wagging her tail. When the girl finally brought the food, she held the tray away from the car, like she was afraid to give it to them until she got the money. Ella handed her a twenty and told her to keep the change, but Brown growled. Then the girl was afraid of the dog. Ella glared at the dog.

"Brown, if you want to eat, you had better lay down and be good."

The dog lay down and thumped its tail and the girl almost threw the food in the window. She retreated as fast as she could, but looked back over her shoulder at

Ella like she thought that she had to be the craziest person in the universe. Brown was all loving and peaceful now, but Ella felt like throwing up her hands and screaming. Instead, she took a long drink of the drink that came with the combo, put the car in gear, and headed back to the store. She had finished both of the small drinks that came standard with the combos by the time they got there. She poured the large coke in a pan for Brown and could swear that she saw relief on the dog's face. As she divvied up the food, she wondered what that girl would think if she knew that her dog drank coke, then she went to work on the root beer.

When every scrap of food was gone, she stocked the shelves and Brown slept. By seven PM, the sale table was full, the shelves were full, the display window featured the new dolls, The mail orders were packed, labeled and ready to go, and the place was spotless. It was also dark and for some reason, Ella did not want to go home. She didn't really have to, because the dog was with her. They drove through the town, which was all but dead and then went home, because there was really no place else to go. She cleaned the house, shampooed her hair, checked out her closet to make sure her clothing was in order, even dug out her make up and placed it on the dresser. She drank a glass of warm milk and went to bed. Tomorrow, she would try to make herself look presentable.

She dreamed, of all things, that she was riding a horse, a big, beautiful bay. They went at a slow, gentle pace, both content and enjoying the ride and the scenery and then they went up a big hill. When they reached the top, she realized that the horse was over tired and she took it into the barn, It lay down and she began to brush and care for it. She was afraid that she had harmed the animal. In the dream, she and the horse could communicate without words. 'Why didn't you tell me you were so tired? We would have stopped. I didn't mean to hurt you.' The horse just looked at her with eyes full of love and forgiveness and went to sleep. Ella knew that she was dreaming, but it was so plain. Her mother entered the room and was walking around, putting something away, picking up things, and looking about. This was strange, for both Ella's parents had died when she was seventeen years old. Mr. Smithers walked in and started assessing the place. Ella backed over to the other side of the barn and knelt before two cages. "Oh! Kitties!" She heard herself say this as she reached into the cage to get them out, and was instantly awake.

It was just a dream, she told her self, not even a really bad dream, still, she felt that it meant something. She willed herself back to sleep and dreamed again. This time, there was danger from rising water and she had a truck parked at the top of a hill. She had two huge, white cats, one under each arm and was struggling to carry them up the hill to her truck so that they could get to safety. She woke up before she got to the top of the hill. She lifted the curtain by her bedside window and looked out to see that it was daybreak. The sun was just coming up.

As she rolled out of bed, she thought that she should

at least be glad that she had slept long enough to dream. Maybe now she wouldn't look so tired when Betsy and family got home. She couldn't shake the dreams about the horse and the cats, and when she and Brown went to the mailbox, there was a magazine with an article about dreams in it. According to the article, dreams of cats meant trouble. They hadn't felt like trouble in her dream. What did that say about her? She had ridden the poor horse to exhaustion, up that hill and found cats. She had been struggling to carry the two big white cats up the hill to safety. Was she heading straight for trouble when she wanted so badly to avoid it? She wished that she knew someone who could interpret dreams, or maybe she was glad that she didn't. She had coffee and cereal, put out dog food and water for the dog, and went to the store. As she got into the car, the dog headed down the road in the opposite direction. Once again, she wondered where it went. When she glanced in the mirror, she decided that she looked human again. Beth wouldn't be back at work for a few more days, but she opened the store anyway.

About ten o'clock, the door flew open and Daniel rushed up and caught her in a bear hug, lifting her off the floor. "You sure are light! I missed you. You should have gone with us. It was so much fun! Grandpa took me to all these neat places. I never thought there was so much to do in Ohio. Grandpa knows everyone." He ranted on and on. Every few words was grandpa."

Ella felt Betsy look her over. "Have you lost more weight?' She heard concern in her daughter's voice.

"Maybe just a little, but I feel fine."

Daniel was still talking about his grandpa and Ella couldn't help but think about John. She managed to smile at him, but he noticed her sadness.

"Don't be sad, Gran, I loved Grandpa John too. It's just that he was always with Uncle Jack, and I'm sorry, but I really don't like him. Bengie would do anything to get their attention and Jac--, I mean Uncle Jack was really mean to him. It was just more fun to hang out with you and Mom. Besides, you had all the cakes and cookies."

"I'm just glad that you had a good time, and I'm so very glad to have my family back. O K, now, what did you get for Christmas?'

"It wasn't so much stuff, it was going places, and eating all that food, and grandpa picking the guitar and all of us singing those songs. He taught me to pick a few notes. I might need more work so I can buy a guitar and learn to play."

"Well, that's good, because I've about worked myself to death." Too late, she realized what she had said and that Betsy now knew that she had not spent the holidays with Sue. It was disappointment, sadness, maybe pity that she saw on her daughter's face and she didn't like it, but what could she say? To her surprise, Bets just walked over and gave her a hug.

"Mom, come over for supper tomorrow, no arguments, and Mom, we're going to go to church soon. Those were the songs Daniel was talking about."

Her family left and customers drifted in and out. She had not expected much business right after Christmas and New Years, but she sold quite a bit of stuff. She worked right through lunch and didn't get home until after dark. The dog seemed all right and it still had water and food, so she went straight to bed. She would start making bunnies again tomorrow. They always sold good at Valentine's Day, especially with hearts and flowers, and they sold like crazy around Easter. Both those times would be here before she knew it. She'd give her precious Daniel and his friends all the work that they wanted. Thank you, Lord, she sighed as she drifted off to sleep.

Chapter 9

She woke the next morning to the ringing of the phone. Even before she answered, she knew that Sue was back. She smiled as she said "Hello".

"Good, you're back. How was Ohio?"

"I didn't go, but the kids had a wonderful time. Daniel can't stop talking about it. It was really good for them. All three of them looked so rested."

"Some how I knew it. You spent all this time holed up with that dog, didn't you. Are you ok?" Sue sounded worried.

"Oh yeah. Are you coming to the store today, or did you just get back?"

"We got home last night. I'll be in about noon. I'll bring lunch, otherwise you won't even eat. Did you eat at all while we were all gone?"

"Of course," Ella laughed. "Hey Sue, you know all those empty buildings around town, where the plants have all moved away? Some of them are kind of small. Do you think that we might rent one, put in some machines and tables and start making crafts there?"

"WHAT? Are crazy?"

"Well, yes, but you've known that since the day that we met. It's just a thought. I'm not at all sure that I want to do it or that I even could. It would be a headache, but you know as well as I do that this town needs jobs. I better get going, see you soon."

Ella put out food and water for the dog and left early. Now that she had begun to come back to life, she wanted to see how Bengie and his brothers were doing. She went to the restaurant to have breakfast and see if she could find out anything, Bengie was there, working extra hours until school started back in a few days. He was smiling as he busted the table next to Ella. As he stacked the dirty dishes in a pan on the cart and wiped down the table, he said, "My last year of school and it's over half gone. My grades are ok. It's for certain now. I'm joining the marines as soon as I get that diploma. The boys practically live with grandma anyway. She says they are a lot of help to her." He wheeled the cart away as the waitress brought her breakfast and refilled her coffee. He hadn't mentioned Jack or June and Ella hadn't asked about them.

She finished breakfast, then drove by her new home to be. To her surprise, the men were working on the fence and she stopped to check on the progress. They were doing a good job and she thought it would keep Brown inside just fine. She went into the house and found it ready for the furniture. Her spirit soared and plans raced through her head. At the store, when she should have been sewing merchandise, she found herself making curtains and spreads for her home. The very next week, she had furniture delivered, computers set up, even bought a newer and better sewing machine. She started taking Brown over every evening to get her used to the place. The dog seemed to feel right at home, but she walked the entire length of the fence. Ella figured she'd move the last of February or the first of March, the slower time at work, between Valentine's and Easter. She went to bed most nights dreaming of sitting in one of the rockers on the porch of her new home, but she was restless tonight. She had a feeling that time was short and wondered where that thought came from.

She wasn't feeling as nervous and jumpy, so she went outside and sat on the hood of her car to watch the stars. It was just good dark, about six PM, She used to do that a lot, just sit and stare at the beautiful night sky and think how truly awesome God must be. This night, the moon was round and bright in the sky. There was a star that she had not seen before just under the moon, like the dot of a clock at the six o'clock position. It reminded her of a clock and once again the phrase 'time is short' crossed her mind. She shook it off and watched the stars for awhile longer. She and the dog walked around for bit, but didn't get out of the yard or driveway. By the time she went inside, the star was at the seven o'clock position. She looked twice to be sure, but she wasn't frightened, just puzzled. Still too restless to sleep, she stuffed and finished bunnies as she halfway watched television. The ten o'clock news came on and caught her attention.

A smiling announcer said; "We've had several calls about what's going on with the moon tonight. It looks like a star is going around it." They showed a picture and sure enough, the star was at the ten o'clock position. "Folks are wanting to know what it is and the truth is, we just don't know." They continued to smile and discuss it as the program went to commercial. Ella glanced at her Bible laying open on the other end of the sofa. She picked it up and read Acts 2:19 "And I will shew wonders in Heaven above, and signs in the earth beneath; blood, and fire, and vapour of smoke. She wondered if this was one of the wonders that He was talking about. She thought back to those oil well fires that the troops had been unable to put out, and how long those billows of smoke had come out of the ground, but it was the thoughts of the blood that made her shiver.

The dreams still plagued her, and she still dreaded to turn on the water faucet. The "Critter" still came to torment once in awhile, but she and the dog all but ignored it by now and it didn't come as often as before. Once in awhile, she could swear that she head a voice, mostly just a word once in awhile, like the time she heard her name. She kept this to herself because she was afraid to tell anyone. As she sat there and thought about moving, she heard only one word; "Hurry." It made her fear for her sanity more than it made her uneasy. Abruptly, she got up, went to the kitchen and swallowed four aspirin with half a glass of milk and went to bed. She left the television on. If she heard anything unusual, she would tell herself that it was the TV.

She knew that she had been asleep but now she felt like she was half-awake. She could hear a roaring sound in her head that was getting louder by the minute. Vaguely she thought 'I must have taken too much aspirin'. She would have gotten up, but her body was just too heavy. It felt wooden. She couldn't move and the sound was getting louder. Now she could see the dark clouds rolling in, getting darker and thicker by the minute, and she could see the wind bending the trees double. They almost touched the ground. She wanted to run, but couldn't. It didn't feel like she was in her bed anymore. She was someplace dark and damp, but the wind wasn't touching her. She thought that she was screaming, but she couldn't hear the sound of her voice, only the roar of the wind and now it wasn't just bending the trees. It was uprooting them. A giant oak slammed down in front of where she was standing, missing her by about three feet. She tried to move back, but there was a hard, cold wall of some kind behind her. Though the limbs, she could see a wide path of trees being ripped and broken from the ground. Pieces of metal and boards flew over and the roaring, whistling sound deafened her. She saw a car roll off the side of a road and keep on rolling down a hill. She couldn't tell if anyone was in it. It was getting darker by the minute and she could see less and less, but the noise kept getting worse and the rain and hail started blowing in on her. She felt something warm and furry rubbing or tugging on her leg and her eyes flew open.

She lay there sweating and shaking violently, unable to speak or move. Brown left her leg and came hesitantly to the head of her bed. She whined a little, then put both front feet on the bed near Ella' head. When Ella could move, she wrapped her arms around the dog and cried like a baby. She didn't even try to sit up, because she knew that she couldn't. After awhile, her cries sounded like the dog's whimpers. She became aware that it really was coming a storm, but nothing like the one she had just dreamed about. She could hear the thunder and see the lightening flashes through the curtains. Brown lay on the floor and Ella drifted off to sleep to the sound of the rain falling on the aluminum trailer and started dreaming again.

In this dream, she was lazily drifting down the river in a huge rubber raft. She felt relaxed as she let her hand hang over the side and drift along in the water. It was getting kind of late in the evening and the sun was low in the sky. She glanced toward it and thought, what a lovely sunset. It was more red than orange but where it shone on the darkening emerald green water, it looked like a shiny orange path. Ella started drifting toward the bank to the place where they picked up the raft. It seemed odd that no one was there, just a few empty rafts that had already floated to shore ahead of her. One was hung up on some driftwood in the edge of the river. It had gotten darker very fast. The water now looked inky black, but the red streak was still visible and Ella could no longer see the sun. Something is very wrong, she thought as she climbed out onto the slick, muddy riverbank and pulled the raft to shore. She slipped and sat down hard on her rump. When she put her hand out to steady herself, she felt a body, warm, but not moving. She got the flashlight out of the raft and bent to check closer. She turned the person over and felt something warm and sticky on her hand. She shined the flashlight on her hand and saw blood dripping from all five of her fingers. She woke up screaming. This time, Brown ran from the room.

Ella finally managed to sit up in bed. She realized that it was already daylight. The sun was shining through the curtain. From the angle that it was shinning in the window, it must be about ten o'clock and she knew that it was Friday, and that she needed to be at the store. She couldn't do it. Her hands were shaking. Her throat was raw and sore. She felt so weak. She was so filled with fear that her body actually trembled. After about thirty minutes, she hung her wobbly legs off the bed and was able to stand. She stumbled to the kitchen and grabbed a bottle of water from the refrigerator. After two or three attempts, she managed to swallow some water, then plopped down on the end of the sofa. When the phone rang, she jumped, picked up the receiver, and croaked "Hello?"

"Oh my Lord! Ella! What's wrong? Never mind, I'm on my way."

A few minutes later sue used her key to open Ella's door and rushed in. She took one look at Ella, walked over and sat down beside her and wrapped her arms around her. Ella cried again then sipped a little more water.

"What is it? " Sue urged. "Tell me what's wrong."

"Dreams, all night long."

Sue gently wiped the hair from Ella's face as if she were a child. "Should I call Betsy?" She reached for the phone and Ella grabbed her hand

"No. Please don't upset her." They sat in silence for a few minutes, then Ella said; I can't go to work today. I don't know if Beth opened the store or not."

"She did, I called there first looking for you. She sounded busy. As soon as you're better, I'll go help her. What can I do to help you?" She was already starting the coffee and taking down pans to cook food. This brought the dog out of hiding and into the kitchen. By the time that Ella had a couple of cups of coffee and some of the soft, scrambled eggs in her stomach, she was able to convince Sue that she would be fine and Sue went to help Beth. Ella cleaned up the place and lay on the sofa. She turned the TV on and dozed off and on, half way listening to the guest on the talk show talking about global warming and trends in the weather and how we could expect more frequent and more severe storms, even tornadoes.

Someone was knocking on her door and Brown was barking. Ella sat up rubbing the sleep from her eyes and went and opened the door, thinking that Sue must have come back. The FBI man that had been in her store stuck his badge in front of her. She waved it away. "Please, I remember you."

She stepped back and opened the door all the way and he smiled as he walked in. He sat on the sofa without being asked and she started a fresh pot of coffee.

"I'm sorry to bother you again, but I think this is something that you will want to know. Say, are you ok? You don't look so good." He was starring at her.

"Gee thanks! I wonder why?" She had not meant to say that out loud and she clamped a hand over her mouth and felt her cheeks turn red. The dreams, the lack of sleep, the stress was taking its toll. She felt like she was falling apart. She had intended to just let him search the trailer, or ask his questions or whatever and get out as quickly as possible.

He shook his head and smiled at her. "I didn't mean it like that, you're beautiful, by the way. I just wondered if you were sick or something. You haven't been out much lately. You were locked in here all through Christmas. You know, that coffee sure smells good, can you spare a cup?"

Ella poured him a cup and took it to him, then she took her own and sat in the chair over by Brown's vent. It was the furthest one from the agent. That chair even looked uncomfortable and he looked at her quizzically.

"I don't bite, you know."

She sipped her coffee. "Never thought you did. Do

you need to search my home now? Do I need to step outside or just sit here out of the way?" She frowned at him and noticed he looked a little tired himself. He also looked a little embarrassed, and suddenly Ella wondered if he'd already done that.

"Ouch!" He smiled and cleared his throat. "Some things that I need to tell you. Jack and Maddie have been arrested, along with a lot of others. They'll get out on bail, though not for long, but I imagine that means more trouble for you. Just remember that after the trial, they will be put away for a very long time. They had this drug ring going on; legal drugs, illegal drugs, you name it." He took another long swallow of coffee.

It suddenly dawned on Ella exactly why he'd ripped her dolls and bunnies open that day in the store. He'd thought that there might be drugs hidden in them. Shock and anger were written all over her face, but he ignored it.

"The investigation was already going on when the police found those drugs and the other evidence in Maddie's car that night that she came here. Maddie had connections down there and Jack had them here. They used John to transport things back and forth." Ella shook her head and opened her mouth to speak, but he held up his hands to stop her and continued. "Willingly or unwillingly, I'm not sure, but, Ella, John was a part of it. He acknowledged the look on her face and glared at her. "You were married to him, for God's sake! We had to investigate. We had to know who was involved. Anyway, he's dead and after I found out that you and your daughter and her family were not involved, I didn't dig too deep. I still may have to, and I will if necessary, but I didn't find where he personally took any of the money. By the way, it looks like they left your nephew out of it. That was a shocker. I thought for sure that he was involved and was all set to try him as an adult. Anyway, this will be in the news, and I'm not sure if John's name will come up or not. Just try to be prepared. You might want to talk to your daughter." He drained the last of the coffee and got up.

Ella still hadn't said a word. She sat there gripping the chair and thinking that this couldn't be true. It couldn't be happening, but now she remembered seeing his car parked by the sidewalk near the store several times. She had also seen him hanging out across the street a few times. It had never even crossed her mind that he might be watching her. She had to snap out of this. She felt like she'd been sleep walking through life. Real life felt like one of her bad dreams. It's a wonder that I can tell the difference, she thought.

"You got a rotten deal and I admire the way you dug yourself out of it." He got up and refilled his coffee cup. He drank a few sips, put the cup in the sink and headed toward the door.

"I'm sorry you got caught up in all this Ella. If federal funds had not been involved, it might not even be newsworthy, but—" He made a helpless gesture with his hands.

"Federal funds? And the drugs in her car?" Ella found her voice.

"Yeah, I told you, this is big. I really shouldn't be telling you anything at all, but I hate to see innocent people get hurt. I didn't tell you all of it, by the way, but these guys don't discriminate, they don't care about anyone. Prescription drugs, street stuff, and of course meth." He had opened the door and already had one foot out when he turned and looked at her again. Haven't you been watching the news, Ella? Haven't you seen all those clinics closed and people arrested, not to mention all the meth lab explosions? One of those happened not twenty miles from here." He closed the door and left. He might as well have told her to wake up and smell the coffee.

"Wait!" she called after him. "Does that mean that your job here is done?" "Will you be leaving soon?" She wondered why she had asked him that and figured he'd tell her that it was none of her business.

He turned and looked back at her. The smile that lit up his tan, even featured face showed those even, white teeth this time. "Nope! See ya" He got in his car and backed out the drive with the window down, singing along with his car radio.

Well, that shook off the effects of the dreams. She took a bath, dressed and went to find Betsy. They talked, cried, fumed, and even laughed about a few things for hours. Those horrible dreams were the only secrets that she still kept from her daughter. She left feeling that they could handle whatever happened with that investigation. She got to the store just before closing time and brought Sue and Beth up to date. They didn't really know what to say, but both agreed that Jack would be stirred up again and would blame Ella. They agreed they would try to have at least two of them at the store when it was open. Ella couldn't help but think about how isolated she was at the trailer.

"I'm moving next week." She announced this abruptly and both her friends turned to look at her. "Brown can stay in the house and I'll walk her if that fence isn't ready.

"I'll help you."

"Me too."

Ella laughed. "I don't think there will be much to it because I plan on donating everything in that trailer to the goodwill or to anyone who wants to come and get it."

Sue laughed. "They can have the trailer too if they will get it off my land, then I'll get a dozer out there. Ella, why not do it this weekend?"

"Well, I have to work. The stock is low again, and Bets and I are going to church Sunday. She asked me if I would go with her back to the church where we used to go. I feel unworthy to even enter a church building, but I just couldn't say no to that request." She got up and started putting things on the bargain table. Lightning flashed in the sky and reflected through the window. She looked out and didn't see much of a cloud, but she heard the thunder in the distance. It was a little early in the year for thunderstorms. The thunder boomed louder.

She would sew tonight and keep the computers cut off. Surge protectors could only do so much. She had always thought of spring as the storm season, but it seemed that they could pop up at anytime now.

As she sat there sewing with radio on, she was unable to stop thinking. John had been dead less than a year, and already, the man who had been her life was barely more than a memory. He was fading away and she was trying so hard to hold onto what she had left of him. She tried to feel the closeness that they'd once had and couldn't. She tried to cry for him, but the tears didn't fall. Her eyes felt dry. She had thought that she knew him so well, thought of him as a part of herself, but he had lived a whole other life, another world, and she hadn't even been aware of it. If she concentrated, she could almost see him now, tall, broad shouldered, and stoic. She tried harder, for she really didn't want to loose what they'd had. Finally, she felt the tears roll down her cheeks.

Women had always been attracted to John, but he didn't seem to notice and Ella had never once thought that she might loose him to another woman. Except when he was doing his sales promotions, pitching his products to the doctors, he didn't talk a lot to anyone other than Jack or maybe Mr. Smithers when he made any kind of business transaction. When he was home, he mostly piddled around the house and yard, watched TV, and relaxed; at least that's what he did when he wasn't in the garage with Jack. He would often walk up behind her and hug her, molding her body to his, while she was cooking or washing dishes and she would gladly leave the chore undone. He had made her feel safe and protected, but now that she thought about it, he could be secretive too. She remembered once, they were going to see a movie and he had boxes stacked in the back seat and the passenger seat of the car. He unloaded them in the garage, and locked the door. When they got back home, the boxes were gone. Ella had noticed it because the garage door was open when they returned and she knew that John never left it that way. When she mentioned it, John just said; "Oh that was just some stuff I brought back for Jack He probably just came over and got it. I'll call and make sure." Ella had forgotten all about things like that. She had trusted him so completely. Now she found herself remembering just how much time John and Jack had spent in that garage. Sometimes, they didn't even let Benjie in there with them.

She thought of the FBI man, so self confident, so sure of himself, and so convinced that John was just another criminal. That first day when he came to the store, he'd thought the same of her. It made her mad, and she would die before she admitted to herself or anyone else, that she was also fascinated by him. John was involved, he had told her, and she knew that he believed it, but his attitude toward her had somehow changed. She realized that he was doing her a favor, trying to keep John's name out of it. She had no idea why he would do that. She forced herself to think of something else. Suddenly it dawned on her that she and her family must still be under surveillance and she couldn't imagine why.

She knew that John's business involved drugs, transporting samples to doctors' offices and clinics, stuff like that. But Meth? He'd never touch that stuff! He never transported narcotics. Those samples were sent to the doctors by mail. There was no way on earth that she could ever believe he would do anything like that. He would cater lunches, even have dinners at hotels sometimes to promote a new product, but a few perks is as far as it went. He might drink a little wine at those get togethers, even get a room and stay over if they ran late or if he was tired, but she just could not make herself believe that he would break the law. She also could not believe that he would have an affair with someone like Maddie nor anyone else. Jack would do it. He would do anything. She found herself thinking that maybe John was just covering up for Jack. They were so different, but then they were always so close. Ella couldn't stand the thoughts running through her head and she couldn't stop them, so, as usual, she went to work.

Chapter 10

Ella started moving her computers from the trailer to her new house. Disconnecting them, packing them in the car, getting them all set up in the new place, making sure that everything worked right, took a long time. She left one sewing machine and some of the materials that she would need in case she couldn't sleep. She had started that project this morning, then went to work at the shop, and after they closed the shop, she went back to the moving. It was Friday evening already, and still not quite dark. She could have finished the moving, but the men were still working on the fence. Another crew was working on the landscaping. She knew some of the workers, but not all of them. She could feel them watching her each trip that she made, and it made her uneasy. She had heard a car turn around in her driveway early this morning when she took the first load inside, and even that made her jumpy. She had her head hung down again as she returned to the car from taking in what she had decided would be the last load for today. Most of the men working outside had packed up and left by now. She opened the car door and was about to slide in.

"Hey, Ella, ---"

She jumped a foot. "Hi, a –" She suddenly realized that she didn't know his name.

"So, you remember me but you forgot my name." He smiled a lazy, insolent smile at her and took a step closer as he watched her face turn red. He wasn't even sure that he'd ever told her his name. A second later, he watched anger replace embarrassment. Her face was an open book. If anyone ever wore their heart on their sleeve, it was Ella. It was a big, kind heart and it irked him that John and his cronies had abused it. She thought that she had it well hidden behind all that hurt and anger, but he was no fool. He stepped a little closer.

"What now? You need to search my car, the boxes that I took into the house?" Ella was exasperated. She popped the trunk and opened the back car door and stepped aside.

He laughed right out loud, even though he tried hard not to. "Just don't offer your body, that might be a little hard to turn down." Then he took a step backwards because he thought that she might actually hit him. He raised his hands in mock surrender and said, "Sorry, I just wanted to be sure that you were alright. It's almost dark and your car wasn't home and that weird dog was huddled up against the door."

"How long are you going to watch me or investigate me, or whatever you call it? I really have nothing to hide."

He just reached into his shirt pocket and handed her a card with his name and phone number on it. " Name's Jeremiah, by the way, friends call me Jeremy. You can call me anytime if you need anything."

He winked at her then got into his car and drove away. It was a cover up, but he was sure that she took it as an insult. He didn't bother to tell her that the down side of his job was seeing innocent people get hurt. It was not a need to know thing, yet he wished he could tell her. This case was getting under his skin. It gnawed at him day and night that Maddie's mother had suffered a heart attack the day that she found out about her daughter's situation and that her father had put a gun in his mouth and blown his brains out while she was still in the hospital. He had no sympathy for Maddie, but her parents had seemed like decent people. Jeremy loved his work most of the time: He really did, and he was really good at it, but things like this sometimes got to him now. They never used to do that. He would try his best to protect Ella. He was getting a soft spot for that kid, Daniel, too. He shook his head. He reminded himself to be objective, just do your job. Changes were coming soon enough.

That night, when Ella saw a car slow and almost stop when it passed her driveway, she told herself that he was probably checking up on her again. She couldn't decide if she was irritated or glad. She fed the dog then started sewing. She sewed all night and most of the next day and used every scrap of material left in the trailer. Still unable to sit or sleep or even watch the television, she packed what remained of the things she was taking with her, leaving out only the cloths that she would wear to church the next day. She loaded the crafts and the machine into the car, then finally fell asleep on the couch, the dog curled up at her feet.

Betsy was there to pick her up as soon as she was dressed the next morning. As Ella slid into the car, she noticed that all three of them were smiling and she couldn't help but smile too. Rob threw his arm over Betsy's shoulder. Daniel let out a fake groan.

"Oh no, they're going to get all mushy again, I just know it." He looked at Ella and they both started laughing. It was so good to see Betsy and her family happy again. Ella settled back in the seat and had almost dozed off by the time they reached the church.

Everyone that they used to know remembered them. There were hugs and handshakes and exclamations. "Ella! You cut your hair, it looks good." "This can't be Betsy! "Oh, I know Daniel from seeing him at school." "My son-in-law works with Rob," They had arrived early and while Betsy and Ella stood talking with a group of women, Rob and Daniel wondered up to the stage where the singers were tuning their instruments. One of them handed Daniel a guitar and asked if he wanted to help them out. They called the meeting to order, said a prayer, then introduced the singers, which they called the song leaders, because everyone in the congregation sang along. Betsy was sitting on an isle seat and Ella was next to her. Rob had ended up toward the back with a group of men that he knew, and to Ella's surprise, Daniel was on stage with a guitar in his hands, picking and singing along with the others. He was really enjoying it and Ella was amazed.

"He learned that from his grandpa in Ohio", Betsy whispered. Ella could here the pride in her voice.

The sermon was about love and forgiveness. Ella wasn't really concentrating, but Betsy seemed glued to every word. Ella caught bits and snatches of what the preacher said as she tried to listen, but she found herself looking around the congregation or getting lost in her own thoughts. Some of it stuck with her, like when he said that Love would cover a multitude of sin, and it pricked her heart when he read Luke 6:27, for it seemed impossible for her to love her enemies, let alone to do them good. He ended the sermon by saying that God loved us so much that He sent His only begotten son, Jesus, to die on the cross for our sins. Ella couldn't imagine a love that great, never had been able to. Oh, she knew it to be true, didn't doubt for a minute that God did that and Jesus loves us enough that He was willing to do it, but to give her child for someone else? Never. She prayed every night for God to protect Betsy and Daniel, to keep them safe from harm and let them be happy.

She couldn't even begin to love someone so much that she would give her child for them. She thought for at least the millionth time what an awesome Being God is. Amazing, wonderful, all the words that she could think of didn't come close to describing Him. As she sat there realizing that she was not even able to comprehend how wonderful the Lord really is and half way listening to the preacher give the alter call, she felt Betsy grab her arm just above the elbow and yank. She looked around to see what was wrong, but one look into her daughter's eyes was all she needed. All Betsy said was Mom-. They were already up and headed for the altar. As she knelt there praying for Betsy, she wasn't even aware of when they separated. Betsy said later that it was the same for her. Half the church was gathered around praying for them, but for Ella, it was only her and Jesus. She didn't even see or hear the others. She couldn't really say much, but she realized that she didn't have to. Her heart and soul were lying right there on the altar and the Lord was healing. Hatred, anger, resentment, and fear were all falling away. It was being replaced with the sweetest feelings of love and peace. She felt so grateful. She raised her head up from the altar and smiled over someone's head at her daughter. That person moved away and she and Betsy just sat there holding each other and smiling while others were still praying, singing and shouting all over the place. After church, Betsy didn't even ask if Ella wanted to go home, she just took her mother to her own house. That night, they all went back to church. The crowd was bigger that night. They didn't get there as early and there was no time for socializing. They all just slid into a pew near the back and became absorbed in the service. It felt kind of like coming home after being gone for a long time. Ella was really enjoying the sermon this time and didn't notice anything else. When it was over, she followed her family out the door, wanting to get home and feed the dog, but Betsy and Rob were talking to another couple and Daniel had joined up with a gang of kids. Ella slipped away from the crowd and over to the car to wait for them. As she leaned against the car, trying to remember if she left the dog in or out, someone tapped her on the shoulder and she almost screamed.

"Sorry, I didn't mean to frighten you, Welcome back." Jeremy stood there smiling at her.

Ella sighed. "Surely you don't think I'd be pushing drugs at church." She just couldn't win.

"Hey, Ella, I really just wanted to welcome you back. I wasn't able to make it this morning. Something came up that I had to take care of but Mom told me you were here." He turned to walk away.

"Wait, you mean to tell me that this is your church?" She had never seen him here when she came before.

"Well, my mom's, actually. She has been a member here for years. I come here when I'm in town, so yeah, I guess it's my church now." He was concerned. He didn't want to keep anyone from going to church, especially not Ella because he knew what she was going through. She was the last person that he'd ever want to put a stumbling block before. He tried to make it right. "My mom is Abby Blacke, by the way. She lives about a mile down the road from where you grew up. I believe that you know her and my sisters. Really, Ella, I just wanted to welcome you back." He left before she could ask anymore questions.

Ella had known Mrs. Abby all her life, and she remembered that she had two daughters. Both were several years younger than Ella, but, for the life of her, she did not remember her having a son. She tried harder to recall him, but all she could picture in her mind was Mrs. Abby and her husband and the two girls. The farm where she and John had lived was in that neighborhood and she had made it a point to check on Abby Blacke once or twice a week until they moved to town. The girls had always seemed happy. Mr. Blacke didn't come to church, and Ella had always thought that was why Mrs. Abby seemed a little sad. Now she remembered that Mrs. Abby had smiled easier and socialized more after her husband died. Both the girls had gotten married right after high school and moved away.

Ella was quiet on the way home, but no one seemed to notice. All in all, it had been a good day. When Betsy dropped her off at home, the dog acted like she'd been gone for a week. Ella put out dog food, scratched the dog's head, and lay down on the couch. She drifted in and out of sleep, worried about her mental status all over again, because for the life of her, she could not remember Abby Blacke having a son. "Wait a minute!" she spoke the words out loud. Jeremy's last name wasn't Blacke. She dug for the card that he had given her. She had thrown it on the table by the phone. Now she thought about calling him and asking him just how dumb he thought she was, but she remembered the events of the day and she prayed instead, then went to sleep and slept like a baby.

The sun shining in the window woke her and as she looked at the clock, she groaned. She had over slept and it was up to her to open the shop today. School was closed for a couple of days. They had to make some kind of repairs and Beth had to baby sit her grandchildren. Sue and her husband had gone up to the mountains for a few days. Ella knew how much Sue loved those mountains. It wouldn't surprise her if they stayed gone for at least a week. She grabbed the same cloths that she had worn to church and hurriedly dressed. As she looked in the mirror to fix her hair and make up, she remembered how much John had liked that dress on her. He had always said that yellow was her color. She would feel better in blue jeans and a tee shirt, but she put dog food and water outside and shooed the dog out and went to work. She would have to work the front, but Monday probably wouldn't be too busy.

About mid morning, Betsy came in and started helping her pile things on the bargain table. "Have you seen Daniel? He was supposed to meet me here at ten. We have to buy shoes. Want to come?"

"Oh no. You feel free to leave me out of that, besides, I'm the only one here today."

"You sure? We are going to Nashville. Just Daniel and

me. Rob's out of town on business. We're probably going to spend the night. I don't like to drive back after dark. Where is that kid? He should be here by now."

Ella went to the door and looked out. The weather was really weird. The sun was still shining, but it felt muggy, kind of humid. Ella could see a few clouds toward the west and she thought she heard it thunder. "Be careful if you go, I think it's going to storm."

"Yeah, but not 'till night time. Another reason I'm not driving back tonight." She joined her mother at the door. "We'll have plenty of time to get there before the rain starts."

About that time, Daniel and Jeremy rounded the corner and came up the sidewalk toward the shop. They were having an animated conversation, gesturing with their hands, faces lit up and alive. Suddenly Daniel grabbed his stomach with both hands and doubled over. Betsy and Ella stumbled over each other getting out the door and running toward him. Both stopped dead in their tracks when he straightened up and they saw that he was laughing. Jeremy slapped him lightly on the shoulder, said something that they couldn't hear, and crossed the street toward the restaurant. Betsy and Ella were both talking at once.

"What in the world? We thought something was wrong with you."

"What was he saying to you? Are you ok?"

Daniel was still laughing. "He wasn't talking. He was singing. A song about you, Gran. He is so funny sometimes. I really like him."

"What do you mean? There are no songs about me." Ella frowned.

"He was making it up." Daniel grinned and sang the words. "Pretty little Ella; All dressed up in yella; Wish I was her fella;"

Suddenly realizing that he was the only one who thought it was funny, Daniel managed a somber look and asked if they were ready to go and if his grandmother was going with them. They soon left but Ella was still fuming when she went back inside to work.

Inside the restaurant across the street, Jeremy sat in his favorite window seat starring into the shop across the street. The pretty waitress flirted with him for all that she was worth as he sipped his iced tea and watched Ella rearrange almost everything in the store. Flirting wasn't working, so she tried a more direct approach. When she touched his arm, he jumped.

"I get off in thirty minutes. Would you like to do something, maybe ride around a little, or go up to Columbia and see a movie?"

"Sorry honey, but I've got to work. Got a few bad guys to round up and a few loose ends to tie." He winked at her and she walked away with a pout on her pretty, cherry red lips. He thought that it ought to be against the law for a woman to walk like that but he sure was glad that it wasn't.

He left her a ten-dollar tip because he felt bad about turning her down then went back to work. This case was about to end. The sooner, the better, he thought. His life was about to change drastically. He was going to live here in this little town to be close to his mom and commute to Nashville two days a week to teach a special criminology class. He'd soon have time to float the Buffalo in a canoe, do a lot of other things that he'd always dreamed about. Oh he knew that he would still be called back for a few special cases, still be a consultant, but finally, he was going to settle down and have a place to call home. Work would no longer be his entire life. He knew it was crazy, but when he thought of home, for some strange, reason he thought of Ella. He realized that he'd been thinking of her since that first day that he'd entered her store and downloaded everything on her computer.

By two o'clock, all his paper work was completed and filed. Everyone he'd been investigating was now in jail or awaiting trial. His boss had called and basically offered him anything he wanted if he would just keep his job, but he couldn't do it. The men who had lived and worked with him for years, were now packing up, getting ready to move on to the next job for the first time without him as their leader. Jeremy felt like he'd just lost his family and at the same time, he felt like he'd finally come home.

Every emotion he had was in turmoil. He had already moved his belongings to his mother's house for the time being. He still couldn't think of it as home. For so many years, he had not even been allowed to visit there. The town felt like home, and he loved being near his mom, but he knew that the house where she had lived with her husband and his sisters would never be his home, only a temporary place to stay due to the circumstances.

Their headquarters at the motel was now a thing of the past. His partner of the last ten years, his number one man, who would now be the boss, had joked that he didn't know whether to call him Andy or Barney, then gotten all choked up and swallowed hard. They had promised to stay in touch, but they both knew it wouldn't be the same.

Jeremy heard a clap of thunder and looked up. Angry looking clouds were rapidly rolling in. Evidently, his emotions weren't the only thing in turmoil today. As he headed toward his mother's house, he wondered if Ella was still at the store. He remembered that big glass window and the display that she was always fiddling with. That trailer where she lived wasn't any safer but there wasn't much of a chance that she'd be there at this time of day. He convinced himself that she would be in her hiding place, the back of her store. There were no windows backs there. She should be safe. When he reached his destination and went inside he told his mom that they should probably head to the basement.

Chapter 11

Ella looked out the window and saw the dark, ominous looking clouds rolling in and felt a shiver run down her spine. She wasn't usually afraid of storms, but she had a really bad feeling about this one. Somehow, it just felt different. She told herself that she was just being silly, there was nothing to worry about. Betsy had already called on her cell and said that they had gotten to Nashville and gotten a room. They might decide to stay more than one night. The weather up there was still good and the weatherman said that there was even a chance that the storms could miss them all together. They might stay too far south to affect Nashville. Now that she wasn't so worried about Betsy and Daniel, she thought about Brown. Oh no! She'd left that dog outside! She grabbed her keys, locked up the shop and headed for the trailer.

It was now so dark that it almost looked like nighttime in the middle of the afternoon and she turned the headlights on. The clouds were coming in fast behind her and she had the pedal to the metal, trying to out run the storm. The car swerved a few times when she took the curves too fast. When she finally shrieked to a halt in the drive, she was calling the dog before she was even out of the car. The dog must have heard the car coming, for she came running up the road from the opposite direction. She came within sight of the car and stopped, like she was waiting for Ella to follow her. Ella called and coaxed, but it did no good. Brown wouldn't come any closer. There was no other choice, Ella could see that she was going to have to pick her up and put her in the car. She started after the dog. When she would get close, the dog would whine and go further down the road. She acted nervous, impatient. Ella was frustrated, but she kept on following, trying to get close enough to catch the dog. Barking furiously, Brown picked up the pace. The thunder and lightning were closer now and really loud. Ella looked up when a few big, plump drops of rain fell on her and was shocked to see how far down the road they'd come. The car seemed so far away and the cloud was now almost on top of them. The wind was picking up, really howling. Even if she caught the dog, she feared they wouldn't make it back to the car in time. She was just about to grab the dog, when it scampered off the bank, still trying to get her to follow.

Ella heard a roaring sound in the distance that seemed

to be getting louder. The wind was blowing the trees in every direction. They were bending so much by now that they were almost touching the ground. The dog barked louder than ever and Ella ran, making a mad dash and lunging for her. The dog slipped through her hands and started up the hill and Ella could no longer see her, but she heard her barking like never before. Then she saw the open space between two giant rocks and saw the dog standing in the opening. She could have sworn that she heard that dog say "Get here! NOW!" A tree fell across the road behind her and Ella dove into the crevice. The dog tugged at her dress, urging her further back and she realized that they were in a cave. Wind whistled through the opening and Ella went with the dog. She feared that she would fall into a pit or something, for it was now so dark that she could not see her hand when she held it before her face. They made a sharp right turn and she felt a rock wall on her left, and open space on her right.

Out of the path of the wind now, she backed up against the rock wall and sat down. She held the dog, now a willing captive, close to her body and waited for her tremors to stop. It seemed like hours. The sounds were muffled inside the cave, but still, it was awful. The roaring sounded like a freight train passing by. Her mind screamed tornado. When that finally subsided, she could still hear the trees crashing. The wind was still blowing and the rain was coming down in torrents. She heard water from somewhere below that sounded like a creek running. Droplets of water fell from somewhere overhead and dropped onto her randomly, but she noticed that it was now a lot quieter outside. She took deep breaths and stroked the dog, who now lay quietly in her lap.

As her tremors subsided, the whistling of the wind through the cave opening decreased. Light began to seep in, but the cave still seemed very damp. She probably just had not noticed it before, but now she desperately wanted to get outside. She could imagine an underground creek rising rapidly and trapping them. Cautiously, she headed for the opening walking on the slick, wet rock floor and the dog followed.

Trees were down across the opening of the cave, but she knew that she could make her way out through the branches. There were downed trees and debris all the way back to the road and she and the dog slowly picked their way though it. She saw that in places, the road was not even passable due to the fallen trees. Ella had never seen so much damage from a storm.

She was cold and wet. Her clothing was in tatters. Her hair was wet and stringing around her face. It was a good thing that she couldn't see how pale she was. There was blood from the scratches on her face, arms and legs. Some of it was dried, but a few places were still bleeding a little. The dog, now very docile, padded along beside her and whined softly once in awhile. Brown was also wet and ragged looking, but Ella hadn't really noticed. She realized that she was probably in shock. She knew that she wasn't thinking straight. In the back of her mind somewhere she thought that she would get back to the trailer, or the car and get warm and dry. Her mind had not yet acknowledged that the trailer and the car couldn't have survived the storm. She trudged along like a zombie, just putting one foot in front of the other, the dog walked beside her.

Everything was quiet now. The rain had stopped and the clouds were almost gone. A big reddish orange sun sank slowly toward the horizon, making the puddles of water on the road look red, almost the color of blood, but Ella didn't scream. She was beyond tired and beyond being afraid. All she could manage was to put one foot in front of the other. She saw a car that was badly mangled and flipped over on its side. Her mind somehow registered that it was hers, but she didn't react, just continued to plod along toward the trailer. She thought that she heard chainsaws in the distance and wondered vaguely if she was hallucinating. Brown's ears perked up and then she barked. They rounded the curve and saw where the trailer used to be. Now there was only a foundation and piles of mangled metal and wood. Sue would definitely need that dozer now. That was just one of the many crazy thoughts that had begun to run through her mind.

Ella sank to the ground and leaned on the trunk of a tree. The dog joined her. She thought she heard the chainsaw again and then the sound of a car engine. She must have imagined it but the car sounded closer. She shook her head, trying to clear her mind. She reached down and petted the dog, then she looked up toward the sky and said, "OK, Lord, I'm ready to go now. I give.

Please just put an end to this mess that is my life."

Somewhere, from inside her heart, or her mind, she wasn't really sure, but she definitely heard the voice. It said simply, "At your appointed time."

A car skidded into what used to be her driveway, and when he slammed on the brakes, the back end slid around to the front. Jeremy jumped out and ran to a pile of rubble. He was frantically dismantling it with his bare hands, screaming her name at the top of his lungs.

Instantly, the dog ran toward him, barking and Ella managed to stand up on her wobbly legs. She couldn't run, she was still moving in slow motion. Everything was so surreal. She could hear other cars in the distance now and knew that the emergency crew was out assessing the damage and seeing who needed help.

Jeremy heard the dog and turned in her direction, and then he saw Ella and started running toward her. When he reached her, he just pulled her into his arms and just stood there holding her. Ella didn't resist. He felt so solid, , so strong, those muscles felt like rock, and he was so warm. She sagged and would have fallen if he hadn't swooped her up into his arms. He carried her to his car and placed her in the passenger seat. The dog stayed with him and didn't miss a step. He rummaged around in the back seat and found a blanket and a big towel. He wrapped the blanket around Ella and the towel around Brown, and then he placed the dog in the floor at Ella's feet. He hurried to the driver's side, started the car, and turned on the heater. Finally, he sat back and took a deep breath. He reached back again and came up with a pillow that he placed behind her head. Ella wondered if maybe he'd spent a few nights in his car and wondered why he would have.

She turned her head toward him and tried to smile, "Thanks."

"You scarred me half to death! You know that? What on earth were you doing out here? My God, Ella, you took ten years off my life." He stopped his tirade and looked at her more closely. Then he spoke more gently. "Are you hurt? How in the world did you and that strange dog survive an F four tornado?" He raked his hand through his hair.

Ella came back to life. "My dog is not strange! She saved my life! I didn't even know that cave was there."

She was a little less pale now, and she was mad! She was feeling emotion! There was life in those big, beautiful brown eyes. He realized just how worried about her he had been. It was not like him to get emotionally involved. He'd never done that before, but somehow, he realized he had done it now.

Jeremy suddenly threw his head back against the seat and started laughing. Poor Brown climbed into Ella's lap and looked confused. Ella hugged her. Jeremy reached over and rubbed the dog's head and Ella glared at him.

"No offense, Brown, Thank God you two are ok."

His hand still rested on Brown's head and Ella noticed the cuts from where he had been digging through the rubble. Other cars full of people had pulled up behind them now, and Jeremy got out to talk to them. His team, of course were the first ones there, but others were right behind them. Ella had rolled the window down and turned off the heat, but she wasn't quite up to getting out of the car. She listened to him giving directions and talking to his men.

"There is a really nice lady who lives on down this road. You'll need the saw, trees are down, blocking the road. I don't know if there are others. I've only been a little past Sue's house. I sure hope she's alright."

Ella stuck her head out the window. "She's not home. She and her husband are still in Pigeon Forge. Hers is the last house, the road dead ends at her barn." She saw the relief wash over him.

A group of men that had driven on past them were coming back up the road. Ella listened as they talked to the others.

"It's the strangest thing," one of them said, shaking his head. "That thing just turned, about a half mile past that crevice in those big rocks. It was following the road, then it just cut out into the forest. Everything looks perfectly normal by the time you get to that big old beautiful house down the road."

Everyone got back into the cars and headed back.

"What about town?" Ella asked as Jeremy slid behind the wheel. "Was anyone hurt or killed? Bengie? The other kids?" She was getting upset now. She was no longer a zombie, she was right in the middle of it. She wondered how she could help? What could she do? She looked frantically around like she might find the answer. Jeremy put his hands on her shoulders to settle her down and Brown growled at him.

"Calm down, Ella, I don't know yet. The power is out. Lines are down. The phones aren't working. Crews are already out working on them, but it will be dark soon. The last weather report that I heard said it would miss Nashville. Your kids should have had plenty of time to get there."

"Yes, Thank God." One single tear escaped and rolled down her cheek. "Beth."

"We'll find out, ok?" He pulled onto the road and headed back toward town. "As soon as I knew Mom would be ok, I set out to find you. I thought you'd be in your hidey hole at the shop. I was about to break the door down when Cherrie told me that you had locked up and headed for home just before the storm hit. I couldn't believe it. I jumped in the car and headed out. What made you do a thing like that?"

Ella just looked at the dog. There was no need to answer.

"My store? The restaurant? The people there?"

"All ok. I didn't see your nephew. Cherrie said that he wasn't scheduled to work today." They reached the city limits. "Do you want to go to the store or to your house?" He frowned. "I could take you to my Mom's house, if you don't feel like being alone." The power was still off, but oil lamps were lit and people were gathered in front of the restaurant.

"No, take me home please, and thank you for rescuing me. I didn't even think to say it before."

"Don't be silly. You knew I'd be looking for you. I hate to leave you alone, but I need to rejoin the rescue team." He pulled into her drive and handed her a flashlight. "I'll check on you later." He started to back out of the drive, then stopped and got out of the car.

"Wait a minute, I don't think you have your keys." He bounded up on the porch, pulled a gadget from his pocket and unlocked her door, deadbolt and all. Brown ran into the house, but Ella stood there gaping as he backed out and headed down the road.

Chapter 12

Ella pulled herself together and went inside. She lit her own oil lamps and candles, then she got her biggest plastic pan and filled it with the bottled water that she always kept on hand and took a bath. When she was clean and dressed in her comfortable jeans and tee shirt and sneakers, she left the dog sleeping on the carpet and walked down to the restaurant. She had gulped down three bottles of water, but was still thirsty. As she stepped up on the sidewalk in front of the restaurant, a car slid into the parking space behind her. Someone jumped out and grabbed her in a bear hug.

"Aunt Ella!"

"Bengie! Thank God you're alright. The rest of them?" She was looking him over to be sure that he really was ok. The car that he had been in had already backed out and left.

"I don't know. I was at Dave's. We tried to go see, but they have the roads blocked and won't let me through. I told him to let me out here when I saw you. He's going back to be with his family." Ella could see how worried he was.

"Come on," she took his hand and started walking the four blocks to Beth's house. She was not sure what she would find, but if Beth was ok, she might loan them a car.

The house was there and lamps were lit. When they stepped up on the porch, Beth opened the door and hugged Ella, then Bengie. Without saying a word, she pulled them inside. Her family was all gathered around that big old table in the kitchen and they headed that way.

"I'm so glad to see you, so glad you're ok"

"You might not be, I have a favor to ask. We need to barrow a car. Bengie is worried about his family." Ella sighed. "I know it's a lot to ask, but mine is gone."

Beth handed her the keys. "You know, I think the road is closed on that side of town."

"Yeah, we're going the long way around. I know how to get there."

They headed out of town in the opposite direction and made a big wide circle on the back roads Traveling slowly and finally came out where the wanted to be. They reached Bengie's grandmother's house first and it was ok. Ella pulled in the drive and Bengie jumped out and ran to the door. Ella was at the bottom of the steps when the door swung open and Jack loomed before them. He glanced at Bengie then glared at Ella.

"What's she doing here?" He directed the question at Bengie.

In the mean time, the two little boys had run out and were hanging onto Bengies' legs, both talking excitingly at once. The grandmother and June joined the others on the porch. Bengie pushed the small boys toward the grandmother and stepped into his dad's face.

"You say one hateful word to her, and I will flatten you."

Jack backed off. Ella quietly went to the car and drove away. The kids were ok and that was all she really wanted to know. She drove on toward town, knowing that she would have to go back the way she had come, but she wanted to know if Jack's house, the one that had once been hers, had survived.

It hadn't. That was where the path of destruction had begun. It looked like the funnel had just dipped down there, taking the house and garage with it as it began it's wide path of destruction. The work crew had rigged lights around the sight. All that was left of the house was a small part of the foundation. Where the garage had been was now a big gaping hole. The homes on either side were left intact, but the path of destruction widened in the woods behind the house. A policeman came and turned her back and she slowly drove the long way back to Beth's house. She hung the keys on the peg inside the door and started walking back toward town , then on toward her house without speaking to anyone. They hadn't even seen her. She managed to get by the restaurant without speaking to anyone and trudged along the sidewalk, bone weary and tired. She was walking along slowly with her head hung down and her shoulders sloughed when a car pulled to the curb and honked. She jumped back.

"Hey pretty lady, want a ride?"

Jeremy cut the radio off. He was surprised when Ella just smiled half-heartedly and opened the door and slid in. Neither said another word until they reached her house. He walked in with her and plopped down on the couch. Ella made a fresh pot of coffee.

"Well," he said to the back of her head, "the case is finally over. They found a secret room under your old garage, with computers, files intact, proof galore. I'm still trying to keep John's name out of the news, but I don't know. I could if he hadn't been so involved with Maddie."

She didn't say a word, but he knew that she heard him. He let it drop. She brought him a cup of coffee.

"Will you be leaving now?"

"No, I told you that. I thought I was moving back to be here for my Mom. She's sick, you know." It was one of those things that Ella should have known, but didn't, but she kept quiet. "I guess the real reason that I'm staying is you." He sipped his coffee and looked at her. He had no idea what she was thinking. "When I think of home, for some strange reason, I think of you, Ella."

"About your mom, Your last name isn't even Blacke."

"Nope. Mrs. Abby is my mom; Mr. Blacke is not my daddy."

He finished the coffee and lay back on the sofa. By the time that she carried the cups to the sink and washed them, she could here him snoring. She covered him with the soft throw and went to the back of the house to her room and closed the door. She lay across the bed fully clothed, thinking. She was extremely grateful for her blessings. Her children, Betsy, Daniel, and Rob, were safe. Her friends were safe . Her nephews were safe. In spite of everything, she had found her way back to God, to church, and a new home. From the way things looked and felt, she was soon going to have a very complicated family, then she thought, 'Betsy is really not going to like this little development.'

Ella felt thirsty, but she had drunk enough water this evening to float a small boat. She didn't really want water, nor coke, nor coffee, yet she thirsted for something. She sat up on the side of the bed and picked up the Bible that lay on the night stand. It fell open to John 4:14 and she read;" But whosoever drinketh of the water that I shall give him shall never thirst; but the water that I shall give him shall be in him a well of water springing up into everlasting life." She read the whole story then she got down on her knees and prayed for a drink of that water and went to bed. Ella was soon snoring. She slept better than she had in ages.

The End